The Evolution of Family...

a Karmic Courage Press * Indiana

Ingénue

a portrait of the film

Original Screenplay by Kate Chaplin

QUANITY PURCHASES
Non-for-profit groups, companies and organizations may qualify for
special discounts when ordering quantities of this title. For information
email kate@karmiccourage.com

www.karmiccourage.com

Contents

Introduction
by Bret Robinson

I jumped at the chance to work with Kate on her first feature film. I had worked with her on two earlier productions, both shorts, and filled the same role on *Ingénue*. I found the experience invaluable.

Kate has taught me more about filmmaking than anyone else.

For other filmmaker wannabes out there, I'll share six lessons Kate taught me:

1.   Be Prepared
Kate is one of the most courageous people I know. She believes in takings risks and embracing fearsome challenges. But she did not just jump in to shooting a feature length movie. She recognized that filmmaking is harder than it looks. It requires a unique mix of talents, skills, and "been around the block" know-how that can only be gained by experience, so she started small. She joined local filmmakers groups, volunteered on other people's productions, and shot simple shorts around the house. One stop-motion series involved a spoon's adventures in her kitchen.

She learned quickly, and before long, she was shooting her own shorts, like *Loss* (2007), *First They Came For* (2008), and the semi-autobiographical *Leah Not Leia* (2011). By this time, she was also doing paid work on professional productions as a Script Supervisor or Production Assistant. As the quality of her films increased, Kate attracted local, state, and national attention as an up and coming filmmaker. She sat for print and radio interviews, taught classes and seminars at schools and libraries, and she and her films began to travel to film festivals and conventions.

By the time I met Kate in 2011, she had the game down pat. Production on two shorts, *Love Dance* and *Home Security*, went so smoothly, she was able to shoot and produce them back to back. So, when the time came to make a feature film, Kate was more than ready for the challenge.

2.   Know your story

Sounds easy, right? Kate wrote *Ingénue*, so who could know the story better? Unfortunately, writers do a lot of their best work at the subconscious level, and they are often unaware of the emotional impact that derives from the subtext of their stories. In other words, they are clueless as to WHY the story works.

Kate's story of a newly awakened clone, created as an assassin in the image of her creator's lost love, could easily have devolved into a string of action sequences and become a faint clone of the great Luc Besson film, Le Femme Nikita. But Kate thought deeply about her story, and realized that its emotional progenitor is more Pinocchio than Nikita. Like Pinocchio, Rosaline is a creation—a young girl who inhabits the manufactured body of a woman whose life has already been lived. It is Rosaline's tangle of identity issues, crippling self-doubt, and the yearning to find validation as a woman that drives the story and makes it so compelling.

It's not a big jump to apply this story to Kate's own journey of self-definition as a writer, a public speaker, and a powerful filmmaker.

3.   Surround yourself with the best people you can find

Filmmaking is the most collaborative of the arts. As a writer, you can sit safely in the dark and build and destroy worlds single handedly. As a musician, your performance is critical, even when surrounded by a band. A director, by contrast, is a manager—she works her magic almost entirely through other people. This requires confidence, a lack of an ego, and solid leadership skills.

A lack of confidence can allow others to take over in various ways and pollute or destroy emotional arc of your story. An ego can blind you to good ideas that come from other people. And poor leadership skills always lead to chaos, and many times to failure. Some avoid these problems by surrounding themselves with newbie's and sycophants. This preserves artistic focus and soothes a battered ego, but robs the director of her best assets— knowledgeable specialists.

Kate recognizes the knowledge, skill, training, and experience that go into each of the many disciplines that surround filmmaking. Acting, cinematography, lighting, writing, sound recording, and editing are intertwining threads, entirely different from one another, but essential to the design of the finished cloth. Kate's lack of ego allows her to defer to the knowledgeable opinions of others when necessary. Her confidence allows her to stand her creative ground when she knows she's right. And her leadership skills keep the set moving, and inspire confidence in others.

4.   Lead

Without Hollywood-style salaries, it can be difficult to keep a film crew together for three days, much less three weeks, especially during a heat wave. Kate did that through incredible organization, effective communication of her needs and vision, and through recognition and mastery of the logistics challenge of crew coordination through multiple locations over many days of shooting.

Kate divided her script into individual shots then organized the shot list by actor, location, time of day, and equipment needs to optimize the schedule. She hired a Unit Production Manager, (Joshua Wooten) to coordinate the delivery of actors, props, food, equipment, and crew to various locations as needed. She sent out comprehensive schedules and call sheets showing call times for each cast and crew member, locations with maps, and approximate wrap times well in advance. And she hired a pair of knowledgeable assistant directors (Michael Williams and Riley Vickrey) to be the heavies when necessary. On set, she communicated her ideas clearly, designated people to perform specific tasks, cleared the set of unnecessary personnel, and got the shots.

Most importantly, Kate had the courage to make decisions. When a police car didn't show up on schedule, she cut the shot. When a park location proved unworkable, she called a meeting, and we moved to a more suitable location with a minimum of downtime. As a longtime crew manager in many work environments, I recognize and respect Kate's leadership abilities.

5.   Feed the troops

Kate and co-producer Amy Pauszek organized the whole community to support this film, and the most visible support during the shoot came in food for the cast and crew. We ate like Hollywood A-listers on every day of the shoot. From hearty staples like pizza, pasta, and barbecued pork, to healthy snacks like fresh fruits and vegetables, to decadent treats like flavored popcorn and cupcakes, Kate and Amy proved that a sated crew is a happy crew.

Ice, water, and soft drinks ate up a larger portion of the budget than originally planned due to an unscheduled heat wave that lasted through the entire shoot. Indoors, we sweltered because fans and air conditioning are anathema to sound quality. Outdoors, we wilted under direct sun in desert-quality heat. Despite the weather, we had only three reported incidents of heat exhaustion due to Kate's constant focus on hydration and shelter between takes.

6.   Go Big or Go Home

When Kate dreamt of a filmmaking career, she had the courage to think big. She organized her life around her dream, jumped in with both feet, and kept moving, tirelessly, for years. When she started making her own films, she didn't just post them on YouTube and walk away. She entered them into film festivals and screened them at conventions. She sat on panels, asked for input, and listened to criticism as well as praise. She got her films out there, and she learned new lessons from each one.

Ingénue follows Kate's recognition that she is ready for national prominence among America's established filmmakers. She asks for no special consideration for the film's microscopic budget, for the "fly-over state" locations, or for her gender. Instead, she has consciously made a film that stands on its own merits; a great story, a fresh vision, and a professional production.

Anybody can shoot a video, but filmmaking is hard. There are a great many skills that must be mastered before a story can be told intelligibly, compellingly, and beautifully through film. But, as Kate shows, these skills, and many others, can be learned through courage, hard work, perseverance, and humility.

Foreword
by Kate Chaplin

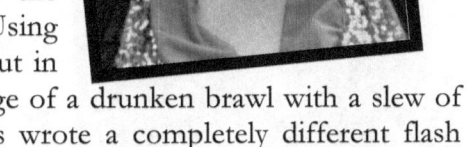

It was March of 2011. I hosted a Death to Writers Block event where we talked about the use of creative triggers. Using music was my usual process but in the workshop we used an image of a drunken brawl with a slew of characters and each one of us wrote a completely different flash story based on the image.

April was soon approaching which meant Script Frenzy. Script Frenzy is a "competition" to write 100 script pages in 30 days with the support of an online community.

During April I was slated to be on a freelance shoot as an Assistant Director but the project was put on hold due to funding. This left my April open to do Script Frenzy for the third year in a row. I decided to sign up without any script idea. All I knew is that I wanted to use an image for my creative trigger.

A random Google search wouldn't help; I wanted something different than the standard creative writing image starters. So went to my friend Brian McGuffog's Flicker account. Brian was an intern of mine and was currently attending NYU and working at the Annie Leibovitz Studio. On his page I saw an image of a young woman lying in cardboard box. I started writing notes:

How did she get in the box?

Where was the box?

Why was she in the box?

I decided to use a married couple with two daughters to be the ones who find the girl. I tentatively titled the script "Girl in a Box" and got to work. That's all I had when I started. I explored the ideas and themes as I typed each sentence. This is unlike me. Normally I do a month or two of research, embed myself in the setting and environment, do character studies, outlines and Hero's Journey layout.

When Carol has her near-breakdown of not knowing what it means to be a woman so she can teach that part of humanity to Rosie, I almost hit a roadblock too.

I would write script pages in the morning and at night I would journal about how I had no idea of how to teach my daughters what it means to be a woman. I figured I would have time to lead into it but Carol's character didn't have that time. She's blindsided and that's what was the most interesting to me.

I didn't set out for the script to be about this big of a topic; I set out to write a strong female character that was found in a box in 30 days. But the question of "how do you teach someone to be a woman," haunted me. I didn't have the answers and something in me was drawn more to the story to find out more about myself and these characters. Many of those self explorations made it into Carol, April, Eleanor or Rosie's characters in later drafts.

After "winning" Script Frenzy (the prize is a certificate you print out and a web badge) with 106 pages in 30 days, I let the story sit. There were many problems with it; it was rough, Carol disappeared in the second act, Richard showed up in the second act like a knight in shining armor rescuing Rosie from some hipster bullies. Richard's character needed to be in the whole film or not at all. Carol needed to be stronger throughout but yet allow Rosie her own choices.

I would only show the first 42 pages of the script to those I trusted. I told them the rest was a hot mess and not ready for eyes, not even mine.

I let the script sit as I had two directing projects line up. I completed the short film *Love Dance* (written by Terry Shepard who is in *Ingénue*) and the short film *Home Security* in four months. All the while, *Ingénue* was stirring in my head.

Come January of 2012 it was time to see if I could fix the script or not. I did what I usually do, research, character breakdowns, and hero's journey. I found the issues and where the story needed more conflict and theme building. I stopped letting the big topic of the story scare me and allowed it to empower me.

I wanted to make a film that mother's could take their daughters to that didn't have a wicked step-mother to overcome. I wanted to make a film that sci-fi fans could take the whole family to. I wanted to bring back the simple sci-fi story like Twilight Zone used to tell.

In doing my marketing research for the film (this is something I do before picking any project) I learned the staggering numbers of women in filmmaking. Only 7% of directors with box office reports were women in 2011. Only 16% of all films are targeted to women when women make up 51% of the population and make the main decisions about ticket buying.

I knew that if I made a film women would enjoy and take their family to, I could at least make back what the production needed to get to an audience. But then a strange thing happened. I found in our reports from our website and social media that we were reaching men and women equally. This proved to me that a good story well told is loved by both sexes.

Ingénue encapsulates what I wanted Karmic Courage Productions to be, a professional production company that tells solid stories that showcase strong, flawed and wise female characters. The great news is we're not done yet. Please support this film so Karmic Courage can continue to bring you great stories you can enjoy though the ages.

The Cast

Melissa Chapman   Raymond Kester

Jamie Angel   Kami Leach

Chris Spurgin   Sarah Moore

David Ross   Glenna Reinhardt

Craig Lemons Tristan Ross Mark P. Jackson

Liz Collar   Amy Pauszek

Why the Title *Ingénue?*

The original title of "Girl in a Box" had to go. It was too horror and too similar to Buried (2012) with Ryan Reynolds.

Kate searched for titles until film geekdom answered her call.

Kate, checking the news of Comic Con, was watching the videos coming out of the convention when she spotted an older video with Quentin Tarantino, Robert Rodriquez and Sam Rami all being asked their advice to an aspiring filmmaker.

Sam Rami answered with, "Make a movie every week. Show it to people and get a response. Learn and make another picture the next weekend."

Quentin Tarantino said, "Make *Reservoir Dogs.*"

Robert Rodriguez said, "Do it in Spanish. Subtitle it and they'll think it's an art film."

A veteran to the film festival circuit, Kate had her answer to give it a foreign-like title so it would fit in the art-film seeking nature of film festivals.

Even though she didn't know how to spell it, she remembered Ingénue, a French word used in the theater for a new actress.

Excited she emailed the Indy Writers' Group (a group she started in 2005) to get some feedback. One writer responded, "I had to look it up, but it's perfect!"

in·ge·nue
noun
\ˈan-jə-ˌnü, ˈän-; ˈaⁿ-zhə-, ˈäⁿ-\

Definition of INGENUE

1: a naive girl or young woman
2: the stage role of an ingénue; also : an actress playing such a role

16

The Script

FADE IN:

INT. BASEMENT - DAY

A soft, naked light bulb illuminates hap-hazard stairs leading down to a dirt floor basement.

ADAM, 40's, a soft-spoken, intellectual man, takes careful steps. He ducks not to hit his head on the low ceiling and exposed plumbing. Beyond the stairs is an open area with MOVING BOXES and misc. storage lined waist high around the brick walls. The primitive basement built in the 1890's is a creepy place. Spider webs, dirt and dust cover the walls, the sound of the furnace and the floor creaks above.

Adam opens a box, then another, then another. He's not in a hurry; he's simply looking for something.

Adam approaches the corner and takes down the first box, opens it to reveal children's school papers. He opens the next box - turn of the century cookbooks. In each box, the items get older. He lifts the box to the side. A large box rests on the basement floor before him. The box is older than the others. Beat up and dusty and no label.

Adam opens the flaps to the box. HE JUMPS BACK!

Shocked at what he sees, he grabs at his heart to control his pulse.

ADAM
(shouting)
Carol! Carol, get down here!

CAROL (O.C.)
In a minute!

Adam take cautious steps toward the box and peers inside. Again he steps back, not believing what he sees.

INT. TOP OF THE STAIRS TO THE BASEMENT - DAY -
CONTINUOUS

Adam stands at the base of the stairs and shouts up the stairs...

ADAM
I'm not screwing around, get down here!

INT. KITCHEN - DAY - CONTINUOUS

Carol, 40's, a strong, but stressed out mother, cooks a grilled cheese
sandwich on the stove top.

CAROL
(to herself)
Can't I just finish one thing around here?

Carol turns down the temp on the stove, but does not turn the
stove top off. We follow Carol into the...

INT. BASEMENT - DAY - CONTINUOUS

Carol bumps her head slightly on the exposed plumbing.

CAROL
Ouch.

ADAM
Come here.

CAROL
I don't have any shoes on.

ADAM
(stern)
Come here.

CAROL
(stern)
Adam, just tell me. I don't have
time for games.

ADAM
Where is that box from?

CAROL
What box?

ADAM
That one in the corner.

CAROL
How many times do I have to say
sorry that this house doesn't have
room for your man cave crap?. I just
told the movers to put it all down
here.

ADAM
But there were boxes down here when
we moved in. Is that ours?

CAROL
(sarcastic)
Does it say baseball cards on it?

ADAM
Was it one of the boxes here when
we moved in?

CAROL
I don't know! Adam, You were the
one that wanted to keep the old
cookbooks and glass bottles.

ADAM
(scared)
Carol, it's real important to know
if that box was here before us.

CAROL
Why? What's in it?

Adam glances into the box.

ADAM
You have to look.

CAROL
Just tell me.

ADAM
(stern and pointing at the box)
Go look.

Carol creeps over to the box.

POV of the Box --> Carol

Carol's head comes in frame slowly. She looks inside. SHE
SCREAMS!

Carol runs to her husband's arms.

CAROL
How did that get in our house?

ADAM
I don't know.

CAROL
What are we going to do?

SOUND of the smoke alarm.

INSERT - grilled cheese sandwich smoking on the stove top.

BACK TO SCENE

Adam rushes upstairs and into the...

INT. KITCHEN - DAY - CONTINUOUS

MIA, 10, stands at the end of the kitchen counter, next to her sister, LIZZIE, 5.

>MIA
>Dad, my sandwich is...

>ADAM
>I got it.

Adam rushes to take the pan off the stove top, opens a window, fans out the smoke.

INT. BASEMENT - DAY - MOMENTS LATER

SOUND of a dog barking in the b.g.

Eerie MUSIC plays over Carol as she creeps toward the box with curiosity. Inside the old and warn box is a WOMAN, 20's, cramped in the fetal position. She wears a skin-tight black body suit that covers her arms and legs. She has on some kind of breathing apparatus over her mouth.

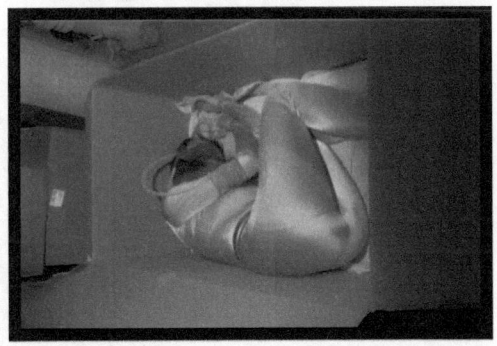

Carol kneels next to the box. She slowly reaches out her hand. She strokes the Woman's arm with a gentle reverence. Carol moves the Woman's long hair away from her neck and disconnects one of the hoses from her breathing apparatus.

SUDDENLY the Woman's HAND GRABS HERS!

The Woman SCREAMS! She sits upright, adjusts her large dark eyes to the light. Still gripping Carol's wrist she stares doe-eyed at Carol.

FADE TO BLACK.

Opening Titles

FADE IN:

INT. LIVING ROOM - DAY

MIA's POV --> The mood is chaotic. Mia watches POLICE OFFICER #1 and #2 talk to the Woman. The Woman is now wrapped in a blanket, sitting on a couch and confused.

POLICE OFFICER #1
Can you tell us how you got here?

Mia sees DETECTIVE RICHARD MILES, 30's, knock on the front door. He nods to Mia before entering.

Police Officer #1 approaches Richard and the two have a private conversation.

END MIA's POV.

POLICE OFFICER #1 (cont'd)
According to the homeowners, they
found her in a box in the basement.

RICHARD
Any estimates on how long was she
down there?

POLICE OFFICER #1
Homeowners have been in the house
for a year. The box along with many
others were in the house when they
moved in.

RICHARD
And they never opened it?

POLICE OFFICER #1
I don't think it's something you
could open and then let sit there
for a year.

RICHARD
Any missing person reports?

POLICE OFFICER #1
None matching her description.

RICHARD
Did you run up the old home owner?

POLICE OFFICER #1
A doctor, Theodore Johnson, died
a few years back.

RICHARD
Contact, next of kin.

POLICE OFFICER #1
We're on it, but there's something
else. She doesn't have finger
prints.

RICHARD
You mean on file?

POLICE OFFICER #1
I mean, she doesn't have finger
prints. It's just a black smudge.
(beat)
I don't think she's human.

EXT. BIG BUSINESS BUILDING - ESTABLSIHING - DAY

Name on the high-rise says "Alliance Clone Corporation."

INT. BIG BUSINESS OFFICE - DAY

In a large commanding office, sits BIG MAN, 60's He's looking
outside though his vast windows. We only see the back of his head
and his dark suit.

A skinny man, 40's, VINCENDS, dressed in suit approaches and
whispers in Big Man's ear.

VINCENDS
Dr. Johnson's #10 has been
activated.

BIG MAN
Send Rune. Tell him I want her
under our control or to disappear.

INT. LIVING ROOM - DAY

Richard sits on the couch with the Woman. The Woman has a
blank stare as if she's sleepy.

Carol and Adam watch from the side of the room. Mia and Lizzie
are snuggled up on them.

RICHARD
(to the Woman)
I'm detective Richard Miles. Do you
know where you are? Do you know how
you got here?

The Woman shakes her head "no."

RICHARD (cont'd)
(to Police Officer #1)
I got it from here. Find the next
of kin.

POLICE OFFICER #1
Roger that.

Police Officer #1 motions to Police Officer #2. The two exit.

INT. LIVING ROOM - LATER

Carol brings the Woman a glass of water. The Woman out-stretches her hand. It's shaky. Richard takes the cup and brings it to the Woman's mouth.

RICHARD
Let's get you to the station.

Door opens - It's RUNE, the voice of the Alliance Clone Corporation.

RUNE
Mr. Ownes, I'm here about your
problem.

INT. LIVING ROOM - EVENING - MOMENTS LATER

Rune sits across from Adam and Carol at a small circle table. A manila folder is in front of him. Det. Richard stands near the table, listening.

RUNE
Do you know the previous occupant
or any living relatives related to
this house?

ADAM
No. It was a flip house. A realtor
bought it, fixed it up, and we
bought it from her.

RUNE
Have you ever heard reference or
gotten mail for a Dr. Theodore
Johnson?

Adam and Carol shake their head "no."

RUNE (cont'd)
Dr. Johnson was a scientist
working with the United States up
till his departure in the 1991. His
last address was your house. He was
working with leading scientists
from around the world to create
human analogs.

RICHARD
I'm sorry, who are you?

RUNE
John Rune of the ACC.

RICHARD
(with a sharp tongue)
The Alliance Clone Corporation. You
guys were shut down for ethics
violations, am I right?

ADAM
Why exactly were you making clones?

RUNE
For study. Scientist were working
for us on a study of environmental
imprinting vs. instinctual
imprinting. Dr. Johnson created
nine Analogs. All of them grew sick
in the lab and died. The one who
lived the longest was raised by a
surrogate family. There was a rumor
that Doctor Johnson created
another. What you found in your
basement was the last human analog
Dr. Johnson created. One made in
secret. One he kept from us.

RICHARD
And you want her back.

CAROL
Wait. What are you going to do with
her?

RUNE
I was told to...

Rune takes out a pistol and places it on the table.

RUNE (cont'd)
...make her disappear.

Det. Richard reaches for his pistol.

RICHARD
That's not going to happen.

RUNE
It has no finger prints. No
identity. It is in fact property,
detective. Property owned by my
employer.

RICHARD
I doubt a court of law will see it
that way.

RUNE
I do have another solution.

Rune motions for Richard to lower his weapon.

RUNE (cont'd)
From all physical aspects the
Analog you found looks human, but
it's not. It's a clone created to
live a human life. I've been doing
this for a long time, and it's in my
opinion it would be best for it to
stay with you. To never know the
truth of what it is, to stay off
the grid, and to try to live a human
life.

ADAM
Hold on a second, you want us to
raise a human analog?

RUNE

We've suspected Dr. Johnson left
some sign of his last creation.
We've been keeping an eye on this house
and...

Rune opens the manila folder to reveal a picture of Adam at age 17
along with a police statement.

RUNE (cont'd)

..we did a background check on both of
you when you moved in. You fit the
profile of someone who would be a
match for this assignment.
(reading)
Adam Owens, born August 31, 1969.
Married grade-school teacher Carol
Stevenson in 1997. Two children
both girls, Mia and Lizzie.

ADAM

Yeah, that's me, so what?

RUNE

At age 17, you were arrested for
assault. The suspect, Adam L. Owens
was accused with assault in 1986
after an altercation with a Mr.
Brian E. Shuler, a machine
operator, in West Virginia. Mr.
Shuler was repetitively struck with
a baseball bat and suffered three
broken ribs and lacerations.

Stops reading.

RUNE (cont'd)

Tell me, Mr. Owens, did you
continue to beat Mr. Shuler even
after the bat broke?

ADAM

I was protecting my mother.

RUNE

So it says here. You were
convicted, were you not?

ADAM

Yes.

RUNE

Tell me, Mr. Owens, does your
current employer know about this
conviction?

ADAM

No.

RUNE

Would it damage your job
qualifications if this was to
resurface?

ADAM

Yes.

CAROL

We'll take the damn baby-sitting
job.

ADAM

Carol!

Carol looks to Adam, then Rune, then to Rosaline.

INSERT: Rosaline is asleep on the couch.

BACK TO SCENE

CAROL

When I was a kid, I used to walk to
school. And every day I'd pass a
dog fenced in the neighbor's
backyard. The dog never barked and
would come up to me, wag its tail,
and lick my hand through the fence.
Some days I'd see the man of the
house scolding and smacking the
dog. I knew it wasn't my place so I
walked on. But one day the dog
roamed into our yard. It was dirty
and had a cut on its leg. I threw
away its collar and I begged my
parents to let me keep it claiming
it was a stray. They knew better and
made me bring the dog back. I never
saw the dog again. I did hear the
gunshot and I did see a fresh
grave. I couldn't help the dog, but
I can help her.
(to Adam)
I need to help her.

Adam reaches to hold Carol's hand.

ADAM
(to Rune)
Is she dangerous?

                    RUNE
         It appears to have the intelligence
           level of a young child. It doesn't
          know how to be violent; it doesn't
          know how to be human. It's a blank
          slate. A newborn in an adult shell.
             What you teach it, it will be.

Rune hands Carol a business card.

                  RUNE (cont'd)
         Each month it will have tests done
               at this office. If you have
           problems, you call the number at the
         bottom. Extra funds have already been
           allocated to your bank account to
         cover the cost of another dependent
           in your home. It should be enough
          for one of you to quit your job and
           stay at home to home school the
                      analog.
                   (to Richard)
           Can I have your department's
           cooperation in keeping this
         information out of the public eye?

                   RICHARD
          For her safety, not for your
                   employer.

                    CAROL
            Does she have a name?

                    RUNE
        We were told its name was Rosaline.

EXT. HOUSE - DAY - MOMENTS LATER

Rune crosses the street.

Richard exit's the Owens' door.

RICHARD
Hey!

Rune turns around. A car passes in front of him. When the car is clear, Rune has VANISHED.

Richard looks around confused.

INT. GIRL'S ROOM - NIGHT

Carol rests along the edge of the entry way and watches as Mia and Lizzie teach the Woman how to play with dolls. The three of them already acting like sisters, giggling and making up pretend scenarios. Adam approaches and puts his arms around Carol.

ADAM
I swear I will never look for old
board games in the basement again.

CAROL
Good.
(beat)
What do we do now?

ADAM
Take it one day at a time. Teach
her as much as we can.

CAROL
Looks like the girls are already a
step ahead of us.

Mia sits on the floor and holds a dragon stuffed animal.

MIA
This is protector dragon. He helped
me when I was sick. Maybe he can
help you.

Mia hands the stuffed animal to Rosaline. Rosaline waits a beat and then cuddles it like a child would. Mia smiles.

                    MIA (cont'd)
            Mom, can Rosaline sleep in here?

                    CAROL
            No, Daddy is making her a place to
                 sleep on the couch.

Rosaline exits the room.

                    MIA
            She's going to be alone on the
            couch, and you know, once, I saw a
                 ghost out there.

                    CAROL
            There are no ghosts in this house,
                    Mia.

                    MIA
            But you didn't know there was a
            girl in our basement. How can you
                say there isn't ghosts?

                    CAROL
                (lightly scolding)
                    Mia.

INT. LIVING ROOM - NIGHT - CONTINUOUS

Adam enters the living room caring blankets. Rosaline sits on the couch. She yawns.

                    ADAM
            It does get a little chilly out
            here. This should be enough to keep
                 you warm.

ROSALINE
Will it keep me safe from ghosts?

ADAM
(shouting to the other room)
Mia!

INT. KIDS BEDROOM - NIGHT - MOMENTS LATER

Rosaline now sleeps on an air mattress between the two twin beds of Mia and Lizzie. All the girls are happy.

ADAM
Good night, girls.

MIA & LIZZIE
Good night, Daddy.

ROSALINE
(copying)
Good night, Daddy.

Adam closes the door and looks at Carol as if to say "that was weird".

INT. BEDROOM/ADJACENT BATHROOM - NIGHT - LATER

Carol sits in the bed. Her reading glasses slide down her nose as she focuses on her laptop.

Adam cleans his face and gets ready for bed in the adjacent bathroom. He talks to the mirror.

> ADAM
> You know what I think is weird? The
> ACC has had the technology to clone
> a human being for decades and hid
> it from us. What else have they
> been hiding from us? What if there
> is a cure for cancer and it's being
> sold to the rich and elite and kept
> from us?
> (beat)
> So one guy went off the radar and
> made his own scientific
> breakthroughs. And we know about
> this but the world doesn't.
> Who's to say there aren't thousands
> of guys like Dr. Johnson, making
> discoveries that are hidden or sold
> to the highest bidder because the
> human population isn't ready for it.

Adam enters the bedroom.

> ADAM (cont'd)
> What if they learned how to make a
> whole meal in a pill?

Carol cares more about what's on her laptop screen than her husband's conversation.

Adam pulls back the covers and slides into bed.

ADAM (cont'd)
(referring to Carol's laptop)
Farkle Addiction, again?

CAROL
No. I'm putting a lesson plan
together for Rosaline.

ADAM
Huh.

Adam kisses his wife on the cheek.

ADAM (cont'd)
Well, good night.

Adam turns off his bedside lamp leaving Carol dumbfounded.

INT. KITCHEN TABLE - DAY

The next morning Carol, resembling an elementary school teacher, collects preschool books from the bookshelves and places then on a large desk in center of the room. She collects a tub of crayons and colored paper.

INT. GIRLS ROOM - DAY - CONTINUOUS

Carol opens the door to find Lizzie and Rosaline in pirate hats counting gold coins.

CAROL
Lizzie, Rosaline, time for school.

Lizzie throws off her pirate hat and rushes out of the room. Rosaline holds up a stuffed doll.

ROSALINE
Can I bring Baby Lady?

                    CAROL
          Let's leave her here until after
                    school.

                   ROSALINE
                   (defeated)
                    Okay.

INT. KITCHEN TABLE - DAY - CONTINUOUS

Eager, Lizzie and Rosaline sit. Carol takes out a deck of flash cards
with large images featuring the alphabet. She holds one card up at a
time.

                    CAROL
               What is this?

                   LIZZIE
                    Ant.

                    CAROL
          What letter does ant start with?

                   LIZZIE
                    A!

                    CAROL
          Rosaline, what is this?

                   ROSALINE
          Bag. Bag starts with B.

                    CAROL
              Lizzie, your turn.

Carol flips up a card with an image of a cat on it.

                   ROSALINE
              (bursting out of turn)
          Cat. Cat starts with C.

Quick shots of Rosaline shouting out all the answers.

ROSALINE (cont'd)
Dog. Egg. Fox. Gift. Hat. Ink. Jam.
Key. Lion.

Carol lifts a card with an image of a check board. Carol covers over the word "Mat." Rosaline is stumped.

CAROL
Lizzie, do you know what this is?

LIZZIE
Mat.

ROSALINE
That's not fair you covered over
the word.

CAROL
So you can read.

Carol takes out a picture book and asks Rosaline to read it. She does with great proficiency. Carol takes "Grapes of Wrath" off the shelf and hands it to Rosaline to read. Again, Rosaline reads without a problem.

MOMENTS LATER

Carol places a tracing book in front of both of them.

CAROL (cont'd)
Rosaline, this might too easy for
you, but let's see.

Lizzie takes her time tracing each letter. Her lines are straight and on point.

Rosaline struggles with the crayon her motion control is not great as each line is shaky.

Rosaline grows frustrated with her work, throws down the crayon, and runs to the bedroom in a huff.

LIZZIE
She has a tantrum.

INT. GIRLS ROOM - MOMENTS LATER

Carol opens the door to find Rosaline on the bed hugging Protector Dragon and crying.

Carol sits on the bed and puts her arm around her.

CAROL
You're too hard on yourself.
Nobody's perfect.

ROSALINE
But you are.

CAROL
I'm far from it.

ROSALINE
But you can read and write and
you're smart...

CAROL
That's not what makes us perfect.
The truth is, there is no perfect,
we all just keep trying.

ROSALINE
Why do we keep trying if there is
no perfect?

CAROL
Because humans struggle with the
idea of being perfect.

ROSALINE
Am I human?

CAROL
I'll teach you the best I can.

INT. KITCHEN - DAY - HOURS LATER

Lizzie and Rosaline help Carol load the dishwasher when Mia
arrives home from school.

LIZZIE & ROSALINE
Mia!!!

CAROL
How was school?

MIA
Okay, now another boy likes me.

CAROL
What about Sean?

MIA
Sean is still my boyfriend but now
Jackson says he like me.

CAROL
What are you going to do?

MIA
I don't know. It's all such a mess.

ROSALINE
What's a boyfriend?

MIA
It's a really nice guy that you
like a lot.

CAROL
And what are our rules?

MIA
(like she's said it a
thousand times)
No kissy-kissy-yuck-yuck and my
school work can't suffer.

ROSALINE
What's kissy-kissy--

CAROL
(changing the subject -
fast)
Let's finish these dishes, girls.

INT. KITCHEN TABLE - EVENING

A spaghetti dinner with a 1950's feel. Carol and Adam are sitting at either end of the table. Mia and Lizzie sit next to each other with Rosaline across from them. It all feels odd and fake. Carol is wearing an apron.

MIA
Why are you wearing that?

CAROL
I didn't want to get my new dress
dirty.

ADAM
Is this sauce from a can?

CAROL
I made it from scratch.

LIZZIE
I like your dress, Mommy.

CAROL
Thanks, sweetie. I didn't think
anyone would notice.

ADAM
Notice, what?

CAROL
My new dress.

ADAM
That's new?

CAROL
Yes.
(taking off the apron)
Oh, who am I kidding? I'm not my
mom.

ADAM
I don't remember your mom wearing
an apron.

CAROL
You don't remember me getting this
dress that you paid for.

ADAM
That's the same dress?

CAROL
(frustrated)
Yes.
(beat)
Let's just eat.

Rosaline shuffles her fork around the spaghetti, not sure how to eat it. She watches Lizzie whose noodle are cut up into little pieces, carefully shoveling tiny bites into her mouth. She watches Mia take one long noodle and suck it up into her mouth.

CAROL (cont'd)
Mia. Don't slurp, it's not lady
like.

ADAM
You're mother's right, use your
manners.

Mia tries to roll the spaghetti noodle onto her fork but it keeps falling off. Finally she uses her fingers to wrap the noodle around the fork.

ADAM (cont'd)
Mia. Don't use your hands.

MIA
I'm just trying to eat.

ADAM
Don't sass.

Meanwhile, Rosaline has a large group of noodles on her fork she tries to shove them all in her mouth. Noodles dangle from her mouth. She knows now not to slurp so she bites down and lets the noodle pieces fall onto her plate. Her eyes scan back and forth to Carol and Adam to see if she did it right.

Lizzie laughs.

> CAROL
> What is it, sweetie?

> LIZZIE
> (pointing to Rosaline)
> She's funny.

> CAROL
> Maybe spaghetti wasn't the best
> choice. Everyone just eat however
> you want to.

> ADAM
> We agreed that we were going to
> teach the girls manners.

> CAROL
> I just want them to eat.

Mia slurps her noodles. Lizzie drops noodles off her fork and onto the floor. Rosaline hovers over her plate and shovels the food in with her fork. Adam shakes his head with disappointment. Carol drinks from her wine glass in triumph.

INT. BEDROOM - NIGHT

Carol sits up in bed, pillows shoved behind her back. Her laptop on her legs. Adam pulls back the covers of the bed.

ADAM
You kind of made me look like an old-
fashioned fool in front of the
girls tonight.

CAROL
I'm sorry. I just wanted them--

ADAM
To eat, I know.
(beat)
I just want them to learn to be
lady like, not savages.

CAROL
They're not going to be savages.

ADAM
You know what I mean.

CAROL
I don't think I do.

ADAM
Don't try that passive-aggressive
thing with me.

CAROL
Why, you invented it?

Cold, angry silence.

CAROL (cont'd)
Rosie called me perfect today.

Adam scoffs.

CAROL (cont'd)
Nice, Adam. You're lucky we don't
have boys; you're no prince among
men.

ADAM
Alright, hold on. What is it that's
bothering you?

Carol closes the laptop lid.

CAROL
We have three girls now and it's
hard. The girls are going to look
at me as a role model, and I'm
not...perfect.

ADAM
No one is.

CAROL
It's just all moving so fast. Mia
has a boyfriend and I don't know
what I'm going to say to her if and
when her heart gets broken.

ADAM
Wait, Mia has a boyfriend?

CAROL
Lizzie is going to start
kindergarten soon. And Rosie, I
don't know what I'm going to do.
People are going to treat her like
a 20 year old and she...isn't.

Adam rubs Carol shoulders.

CAROL (cont'd)
I just thought I'd have more time.
I mean, my mother never wore make
up, we never played dolls, I didn't
even know how to braid hair until I
went to summer camp.
(beat)

Numbers, letters, learn to spell, I
can teach that. Hold your head high
in a crowd...I can't even do that.

ADAM
You're the smartest woman I know.
And sometimes the meanest.

Carol touches Adam's hand in reassurance.

CAROL
I'm sorry. I really am. I love you.

ADAM
I love you--

CAROL
(flustered)
But I don't know what it means to
be a woman anymore!

ADAM
I think you're over-thinking this.

CAROL
It used to be motherhood or career.
My mom chose motherhood. I chose
both, and I feel like I suck at
both.

ADAM
You don't.

CAROL
As a kid in by the lake--

ADAM
--The hippie communion.

                    CAROL
                     Stop.
                    (beat)
        Mom and dad raised me more in the
         hands-off mode and let me just find
            myself and what I wanted to do.

                     ADAM
          And there is nothing wrong with
                     that.

                    CAROL
           But I don't know who I am!

                     ADAM
          You are a giving wife, a loving
        mother, and a loyal daughter. What
              more do you need?

                    CAROL
          I don't know...Something. I feel
         like I can't give to our girls what
                  I don't have.

EXT. PARK - DAY

Carol sits on a park bench and watches as Rosaline and Lizzie play
on the park equipment.

APRIL, 30's, resembling the perfect mom with unblemished skin,
long healthy hair and a model build, arrives at the park and waves to
Carol. Next to April is her son ALEX, 4, who runs off to play on
the swings.

                    APRIL
             (approaching Carol)
          Lizzie sure is getting big.
                    (beat)
          Is that her? She looks like the
                    nanny.

                                                        51

(beat)
Terrible thing about both her
parents. Good thing she has such
a great Aunt.

CAROL
(lying)
Yup.

APRIL
How are the girls handling having a
new sister?

CAROL
Good.

APRIL
How are you handling having
another?

CAROL
Not good.
(beat)
Honestly, April, I'm a mess.

APRIL
What is it? Is it Adam?

CAROL
No, not really, Adam is Adam. I'm
just person soup.

APRIL
What?

CAROL
It was in a magazine...You know
when a caterpillar forms a cocoon
and then goes through the
metamorphosis of turning into a

butterfly? Well the caterpillar
doesn't just sprout wings and poof
it's a butterfly, it actually melts
down into a caterpillar soup and
then from that gook it reforms into
a butterfly.

APRIL
So you're in a metamorphosis?

CAROL
Yes.

APRIL
You really think this is the right
time for this?

CAROL
No.

APRIL
You going pre-menopausal?

CAROL
No! I'm not that old.

APRIL
We're the same age.

CAROL
No we're not. You're much younger
than me.

APRIL
Actually darling, I'm two years
older.

CAROL
And you look like...and I look
like...Now I'm worse.

APRIL
What's got you person soup?

CAROL
It's a huge change now having a
young adult in the house. I was so
comfortable in the toddler phase.

APRIL
You've been taking it school
quarters at time, haven't you?

CAROL
Yeah, I guess I didn't plan ahead
to those transition years from
childhood to adult. I mean, how do
you teach that?

APRIL
Some people never really grow into
adulthood.

CAROL
And I don't want my kids to be that
way. I want them to be confident
and mature women, but I don't
know...what was the advice your mom
gave you on womanhood.

APRIL
Wow. Um...I guess to always have my
best face, to dress nice for the
occasion.

Carol points to her loosely pulled together outfit.

APRIL (cont'd)
Have manners, don't swear - was a
big one of her's.

CAROL
Adam and I are big on that one.

APRIL
Um...Be educated but don't come off
like a know it all. Always laugh at
a man's joke even if it's not
funny, be subtle and ooze elegance.
And there was something about never
leaving the house without lipstick.

CAROL
My mom never taught me any of that,
you're lucky I didn't come here in
stretch pants with holes in them.

APRIL
My mom just wanted us to be classy
ladies. Find a husband, have kids
and then...

CAROL
And then. That's the part I'm
having trouble with. I want to
teach the girls that that is not
all it is to be a woman.

APRIL
That's a tuff one. can't you just

teach them to ride a bike or
something.

CAROL
What about Alex? Is Ben all about
teaching him to be a gentleman?

APRIL
Come to think of it, we never
talked about it.

CAROL
Adam thinks I'm over-thinking this.

APRIL
I don't think so. I struggle with
Alex. I don't understand his
destructive and chaotic nature, but
I love him and I want him to be who
he is.

CAROL
What did you want to be when you
grew up?

APRIL
A model. I wanted to grace the
cover of Vanity Fair.

CAROL
Why'd ya quit?

APRIL
Honestly I got sick of the way
they'd pose me as a submissive
victim. Like my hands for example,
I could never grab an object and
command it, I had to cradle it or
delicately point to it. I had to
touch my neck, like it was about to

fall off. It wasn't fun; it wasn't
what I wanted. I lost it over a
photographer wanting me to be
more sexy holding a bottle of
soap. I mean it's soap, it's get you
clean. And they wanted some
fantasy of a woman feeling like a
goddess just because she had a soap
bottle in her hands.

CAROL
Never really thought about it that
way.

APRIL
So I quit. Got married and had
Alex.

CAROL
Do you like staying home?

APRIL
It's different.

EXT. PARK - PLAYGROUND - DAY

Rosaline, Lizzie and OLDERBOY, 6, are at the base of the stairs.
Olderboy cuts in front of Rosaline.

ROSALINE
Hey, no fair.

Olderboy reaches the top and pushes Rosaline off the stairs.

LIZZIE
No!!

Rosaline falls to the ground and hit her head.

Mothers rush to the scene.

                         CAROL
                        (frantic)
              Rosie, are you okay? It's okay. I'm
              sorry, honey. I should have been
              watching you more. What hurts?

                         LIZZIE
                 Mean boy pushed her.

Carol looks at the blood on Rosaline's fingers.

                        ROSALINE
                      What's that?

                         CAROL
              Blood, honey. You got scratched up
                      pretty bad.

                        ROSALINE
                 (freaking out nearly
                  hyperventilating)
              I don't know what I did wrong.

                         CAROL
              Rosaline. Don't beat yourself up.

Rosaline looks confused with the word play. Carol helps Rosaline to
her feet.

INT. CAR - DAY - MOMENTS LATER

Rosaline sits in the back seat next to Lizzie. Rosaline tries not to
cry.

EXT. HOUSE - DAY

The family car pulls up the house. Mia is walking toward the house,
apparently off from school.

EXT. CAR/BACK DOOR OF HOUSE - CONTINUOUS
Rosaline exits the car in a rush.

ROSALINE
Mia!!!

Carol exits the car and gets Lizzie.

CAROL
(shouting after Rosie)
How's your ouchy? Do want your ice
pack?

ROSALINE
No, I'm fine.

INT. GIRLS BEDROOM - CONTINUOUS

Mia pulls a teen magazine out of her backpack.

MIA
Look what Carrie gave me today.

The girls look at the photographs in the
magazine of young when in grown up poses.
Heads tiled to the side, standing on one leg,
overly laughing, make up overdone. The
girls try to mimic the poses.

INT. KITCHEN TABLE - LATER THAT NIGHT

The camera pans around the table. Lizzie, Rosaline and Mia all have
apparently done each other's make up to an extreme. Carol and
Adam try to not say anything.

MIA
Can I be excused?

ADAM
Yes, Miss Manners you can.

LIZZIE & ROSALINE
Me too?

ADAM
Yes.

The girls run off.

INT. KITCHEN SINK - MOMENTS LATER

Carol and Adam are loading the dishwasher.

CAROL
I'm sorry about last night.

ADAM
I am too. Are you feeling better?

CAROL
I had a nice talk with April.

ADAM
How's April?

CAROL
She's good.

ADAM
I heard an interesting NPR story
this morning.

CAROL
Hum.

ADAM
It was about how the teenage brain
is not fully grown yet. Turns out
the crucial part of the brain, the
frontal lobes are not fully
connected. The frontal lobes are
the part that allow the reasoning
of "is this a good idea." I mean
they have that of course, but it's
just slower. They lack enough white
matter to connect the nerve cells
to the area.

CAROL
And you're thinking...

ADAM
We need to keep this in mind with
Rosaline. She may have the physical
brain size of an adult, but how do
we know if it's fully connected and
matured? You said yourself her
motor reflexes weren't that great.

Carol makes a motion for Adam to look behind him. Rosaline
stands there having heard the conversation. Hurt, she cries and runs
out of the room.

INT. DOCTOR'S OFFICE - DAY

Rosaline goes through a comprehensive physical exam in cold and sterile environments. Neither the COLD DOCTOR nor the COLD NURSE talks to her or shows any bed side manner.

INT. WAITING ROOM/DOCTOR OFFICE - LATER - DAY

Carol sits in the waiting room nearly finished reading a hefty book. Rosaline exits the door, her face solemn, her arms crossed in front of her. Carol catches sight of Rosaline and quickly approaches her.

> CAROL
> Rosaline, sweetie. Are you all
> done?

Rosaline nods.

> CAROL (cont'd)
> Are you okay?

Rosaline's bottom lip quivers trying to hold back tears.

> CAROL (cont'd)
> What did they tell you?

> ROSALINE
> Nothing. They didn't talk to me.

> CAROL
> Hold on.

Carol approaches the large glassed off partition to the SECRETARY.

> CAROL (cont'd)
> Do I need to sign anything to get
> her results?

SECRETARY
For her? No you don't get any
results.

CAROL
Excuse me. I'm her mother.

SECRETARY
(whispering)
We both know that's not true. So
let's not make a scene.

ROSALINE
Mom, let's just go.

CAROL
(defensive)
Wait one second. Make a scene? What
did you do to her? I have a right
to know.

The Secretary picks up the phone.

SECRETARY
(to the phone)
Security, we have a problem...

ROSALINE
It's okay, I just want to go.

CAROL
(to the secretary)
Problem? I'm not the problem. You
not treating my daughter like a
human being is the problem.

The Secretary bites her lip and rolls her eyes knowing the truth of
Rosaline. Two SECURITY MEN in black suits enter the waiting
room.

ROSALINE
(yelling)
I want to go home.

CAROL
(to the Secretary)
This isn't over.

Carol gathers her things, puts her arm around Rosaline, and exits.

INT. LIVING ROOM - EVENING

Rosaline sits on the couch with a blanket around her. She cuddles Protector Dragon and her doll. She stares blankly ahead.

Carol paces in front of her. She talks into her cell phone.

CAROL
(to the phone)
Rune, this is Carol Ownes, you said
to call if we had a problem, and we
have a problem. I want to see the
results of Rosie's tests.

RUNE (V.O.)
The information is for ACC eyes
only.

CAROL
I understand, however you have
placed her in my care and as her
caregiver, I have a right to know.
If she is not performing in a
certain area of physical or mental
abilities, I need to know.

RUNE (V.O.)
It's just not in my control.

CAROL
Make it in your control or I won't
take her back to that hospital. Do
you hear me?

Carol hangs up the phone and cuddles with Rosaline. Carol strokes
her hair in effort to comfort her.

CAROL (cont'd)
It's okay, sweetie. I'll make sure
they don't scare you again.

INSERT - MIA jealously watches.

EXT. SIDEWALK/RESIDENTIAL NEIGHBORHOOD - DAY

Rosaline walks a small black and white dog. She carries her doll
with her. Mia walks with her kicking stones along the way.

ROSALINE
Mom was saying you won an award for
writing.

MIA
(snooty)
You would know.

ROSALINE
What does that mean?

MIA
Nothing.

ROSALINE
Did I do something wrong?

MIA
You and my mother just spend a lot
of time together, that's all.

ROSALINE
Your mother?

MIA
Face facts, Rosaline, she's not
your mother. She's just stuck with
you.

ROSALINE
Stuck with me?

SOPHIA, 10, appears up the street. She waves to Mia.

MIA
Sophia!

Mia and Sophia run up to each other.

SOPHIA
Can you play?

MIA
Sure.

SOPHIA
Do you need to ask your nanny?

MIA
She's not my nanny, my parents just
found her in a box.

SOPHIA
What?

MIA
It's not a big deal; let's go play
on your trampoline.

SOPHIA
(to Mia, whispering)
Why does she have a doll?

Rosaline stands defeated having heard the entire conversation.

Mia and Sophia run off. Mia doesn't give Rosaline a second glance, Sophia, however, does.

Rosaline looks down at the ground in shame.

EXT. HOUSE/BACK DOOR - DAY - MOMENTS LATER

Rosaline opens the trash can and throws away her doll.

EXT. CITY HALL - DAY

Angry PROTESTERS surround the City Hall with signs saying "No Analogs" "Down with the ACC," "We Need Soldiers, not Killers"

Vincends, Big Man and Rune exit City Hall. Rune and Vincends try to clear a path through the Protesters to get Big Man out of there and to the car parked on the street. Big Man gets a microphone shoved in his face.

REPORTER LISA
What do you have to say about the
serious amounts of ethic violations
brought against the ACC?

BIG MAN
I think the people will find we are
in no violation any more than
Dmitri Belyaev was with his
domestication of silver foxes.

REPORTER LISA
You're comparing wild animals to
hardened criminals?

REPORTER #2
Is it true that you got Charles
Manson's DNA and making a clone of
him to be a soldier in this New
Army?

BIG MAN
Soon the people will see that the
ACC has the best intentions for
helping keeping our planet safe by
creating a New Army to do the job
that...you Lisa, don't wanna do.

Vincends, Rune and Big Man approach the car. Rune is the last to
enter the car when something catches his eye.

INSERT --> Detective Richard Miles stands across the street
staring down Rune.

INT. KITCHEN TABLE - DAY

Rosaline and Lizzie are seated at "school." Carol sits across from
them, balancing the checkbook.

Rosaline reads Chronicles of History. A large newspaper like
almanac. Lizzie is doing worksheet pages.

INSERT - 1869 page
CU on the article "Drive for Women's Rights in Britain." Line
reads: "they would no longer be classed with children and lunatics,

as incapable of taking care of themselves or others, and needing that everything should done for them."

BACK TO SCENE

> ROSALINE
> Mom, can I get this book?

> CAROL
> What book, honey?

> ROSALINE
> The Subjection of Women.

> CAROL
> Sure.

SOUND OF A KNOCK at the front door.

> CAROL (cont'd)
> Lizzie, can you get ready for
> ballet?

Lizzie nods and both Lizzie and Rosaline head into their room.

INT. FRONT DOOR - DAY - CONTINUOUS

Carol opens the door to see Detective Richard.

> CAROL
> Detective Miles, what brings you
> by?

> RICHARD
> Please, call me Richard. I don't
> want to bother you, but I was
> wondering if you had a minute?

> CAROL
> Sure. Come on in.

RICHARD
How is she --

CAROL
Rosie? She's good.

RICHARD
Have you been watching the news
about the ACC?

CAROL
We don't watch the news.

RICHARD
The ACC has been taking the DNA
from hardened criminals and
cloning, for lack of better word,
killers. They are growing an Army.
Trained killers under the control
of the ACC.
(beat)
Has Rosaline ever shown any
hostility or sudden anger?

CAROL
No, not a bit.

RICHARD
I didn't think so. So I did some
diggin' on your scientist. I have
that he was born in 1908 in Germany.
Moved to Chicago joined the staff
of the University. He was married
to a Gracie Fredricks who died
around 1970. He had a son.

ROSALINE (O.S.)
Is he still alive?

CAROL
Rosie, how long were you listening?

ROSALINE
I'd like to meet his son, if he's
still alive. If I'm not a killer,
I'd like to know what I am.

CAROL
We can't.

ROSALINE
Please.

CAROL
(to Richard)
Can you keep her safe?

RICHARD
Yes, ma'am, I can.

CAROL
Keep her out of public places, have
her back before dark, and don't
ever call me Ma'am.

EXT. HOUSE - DAY

BERG JOHNSON, 60, gruff, opens the door.

RICHARD
I'm looking for Berg Johnson.

BERG
You've found him.

RICHARD
I wonder if I could talk to you
about your father, Dr. Theodore
Johnson?

BERG
I'd wish you wouldn't.

Berg, takes one look at Rosie and recalls something painful.

INT. HOUSE/KITCHEN TABLE - DAY - MOMENTS LATER

Berg sits across from Rosaline and Richard.

BERG
I didn't really know my father. He
came and left as he pleased. When I
was about seven he left for good.

RICHARD
And that was about what year?

BERG
1959.

RICHARD
Do you know what caused him to
leave?

BERG
Who knows, didn't like mom's
cooking, hated Chicago, found
another job, it was probably a
bunch a stuff, but I think it was

because of that Rosalind woman.

ROSALINE
Excuse me?

BERG
(to Rosaline)
You know what I'm talking about.

RICHARD
Rosalind, who?

BERG
Rosalind Franklin. She was from
England or some hoity-toity place.
She drank tea and worked for some
university that was working on DNA.

RICHARD
(thinking out loud)
DNA, late 1950's.
(to Berg)
You aren't talking about Cambridge
and Watson and Crick are you?

BERG
Yeah, that's them.

RICHARD
What did Rosalind have to do
with it?

BERG
She was the x-ray person or
something and found the structure
for the old two yahoo's to find the
"blueprint of life" or whatever.

RICHARD

And you think your dad left because
of her?

BERG

Yeah. She was visiting the states
for a summer, and that's all it
took. I thought he'd come back once
she died, but he didn't.

Berg stands up and heads toward an old picture on the wall of
possibly his mother.

ROSALINE

Died?

BERG

Yeah, died in 1958.

Berg takes the picture off the wall; something is taped to the back
of the frame. He sits back down at the table.

ROSALINE

If she died in 1958, why did he
leave one year later?

BERG

My father was crazy. Sure a
genius, but crazy, he said he was
going to bring her back. Now that I
see you, I guess he did.

Berg hands Rosaline a picture of Rosalind Franklin, though a 1950's
looking picture, the two look identical.

RICHARD

We were told there were 10 Human
Analogs, like Rosaline. Do you know
anything about your father's
experiments?

BERG

No. Once he left, I didn't give a
damn what he did with his life.
(to Rosaline)
I apologize for my abrupt tone.
(beat)
I did hear that he made a clone of
me, that died. The fool couldn't
foster a relationship with me, I
guess so he made a...

Rosaline nods in understanding.

RICHARD

You know nothing about his time in
Noblesville, do you?

BERG

I'm sorry, I don't. He left ma and
me. My guess he wanted nothing to
do with us, so I want little to do
with him, if you know what I mean.

EXT. HOUSE - DAY - LATER

Rosaline and Richard head back to their car.

RICHARD

I'll get someone on this Rosalind
Franklin.

ROSALINE

(looking back at Berg)
He's in a lot of pain.

Rosaline touches Richards's arm to give her a minute. Rosaline
heads back to Berg watching from the door step. The two share a
private moment. From the body language we can assume that
Rosaline is apologizing. Rosaline touches Bergs arm before heading
back to Richard and the car.

INT. CAR - DAY - CONTINUOUS

Rosaline looks out the window - nearly defeated.

Richard looks to Rosaline. Worried about her, he puts his hand on her knee.

Rosaline looks at a picture of Dr Johnson. Then a picture of Rosalind.

EXT. HOUSE - EVENING - LATER

Richard walks Rosaline to her front door. Rosaline, still a little solemn from the trip, tries to open the front door. It's locked.

> ROSALINE
> I guess Mom's not home yet.

They sit on the couch on the porch.

> RICHARD
> What are you going to tell Adam and
> Carol?

> ROSALINE
> That I'm not a killer but a marriage
> wrecker.

> RICHARD
> That's not what you are. That's
> what you were made from. Okay that
> sounds worse. I haven't spent that
> much time with your new family, but
> I can see they care about you, and
> love you.

ROSALINE
But how long till I become "her?"

RICHARD
Who's to say you ever will? You get
the chance to be and do whatever
you want.

ROSALINE
I just want to be human.

RICHARD
You are.

ROSALINE
I'm not.

RICHARD
What separates you from everyone
else?

ROSALINE
I was born in a lab.
(beat)
Created by a mad-man who couldn't
deal with real people so he made
puppets of them.

RICHARD
You're nobody's puppet.
(beat)
I think you need to get out more.
Be around more people, you'll see
you're not that different.

Adam opens the door.

ADAM
Detective? Rosie? Is there a
problem?

RICHARD
No. Sir.

ADAM
I saw your car--

RICHARD
Mrs. Ownes said it would be okay if
I took Rosaline out.

ADAM
Huh. Carol said this was okay?

RICHARD
Actually I was wondering if I could
take Rosaline out again.

ADAM
A date?

Rosie's face lights up.

RICHARD
Get her out among people.

ADAM
You mean a date.

RICHARD
Not really, Sir.

ROSALINE
I think it's a good idea, dad.

Rosaline enters the door.

ADAM
(to Rosie)
I bet you do.

                    (to Richard)
         Let me talk this over with Carol.

                  ROSALINE (O.S.)
                    (excited)
              I have a boyfriend!!!

Richard smiles.

                       ADAM
            Yeah, we're gonna have to talk
                    about this.

INT. LIVING ROOM - DAY

Rosaline sits on the couch reading "The Subjection of Women" by
John Stuart Mill.

SOUND of: The door bell.

Carol approaches and opens the door to reveal ELEANOR, 30, 8
months pregnant, lovable round face.

                      CAROL
                      Ellie!!

The two hug, as best they can with Eleanor's baby bump.

                  CAROL (cont'd)
            Come in, come in, get off your
                      feet.

                    ELEANOR
            I don't mind. I feel like I sit
              most of the day anyway.

                      CAROL
                   Ankle swell?

ELEANOR
Painfully, so.

CAROL
Mr. Banes is letting you sit during
class?

ELEANOR
I got a student teacher. She's been
taking over during these last
months.

CAROL
How much longer?

ELEANOR
27 more school days. 50 days before
baby.

ROSALINE
Baby?

The women turn their attention to Rosaline, who although has her
book open, has been eagerly listening to the women's conversation.

CAROL
Rosaline, I'm sorry, this is
Eleanor James. She teaches at the
school, I used to teach at.

ROSALINE
And she's going to have a baby?

ELEANOR
At this point, I'm hoping sooner
than later.

Eleanor holds her stomach.

ELEANOR (cont'd)
Seems like the baby thinks my
kidneys are a boxing bag.

ROSALINE
What do you mean? You can feel the
baby?

ELEANOR
Sure, come here.

Rosaline approaches. Eleanor guides Rosaline's hand to her belly.
Finding the right spot...

ELEANOR (cont'd)
There. Do you feel anything?

ROSALINE
No.

ELEANOR
Sometimes it's like bubbles. She's
moving around a lot today so you
might feel a tiny--

Rosaline feels a kick. She giggles in the discovery.

ROSALINE
The baby kicked me! Well you know
not really kicked me, but...kicked
me.

Eleanor is amused by Rosaline.

ROSALINE (cont'd)
The baby can hear us, right?

ELEANOR
Oh yeah.

Rosaline puts her face by Eleanor's belly.

ROSALINE
Baby, please stop kicking your
mommy. She's nice and it hurts
sometime. Thank you. This is
Rosaline, by the way.

Eleanor puts her finger up as if she's waiting for something.

ELEANOR
I think she listened to you. She
must like you Rosaline. Good work.

Eleanor winks at Carol, and school teacher trick to have children
feel good about themselves.

CAROL
I have something for you.

ROSALINE
Can I come too?

Carol nods as the women head to the....

INT. KITCHEN - DAY - CONTINUOUS

On the kitchen island is a pink gift bag overflowing with pink tissue paper.

Carol hands the gift to Eleanor who opens it to find a baby bathtub with soaps and lotions.

                    ELEANOR
               Thank you!

                    ROSALINE
               What is it?

                    CAROL
               It's a bathtub for the baby.

                    ROSALINE
          Why can't the baby use the regular
                    bathtub?

                    CAROL
          Because babies are little and a
               bathtub is very big.

Rosaline looks confused.

                    ELEANOR
          Don't worry. With a great gift like
          this, the baby will be fine. Thank
                  you, Carol.

                    ROSALINE
          Why do they need all this?

                    ELEANOR
          Babies have delicate skin and need
               special lotions.

ROSALINE
Huh. Do they need lots of stuff?

ELEANOR
(joking)
Oh yeah. Find a rich husband,
Rosaline.

CAROL
(to Eleanor)
So are you nervous about the
delivery?

ELEANOR
I'm at the point where I want this
baby out of me, but then
again...How long were you in labor
with your girls?

CAROL
12 hours for Mia, 6 for Lizzie.

ELEANOR
Did you get the epidural?

CAROL
I tried to be strong as long as I
could, but, yes. I don't know what
hurt worse, the epidural or the
delivery.

ELEANOR
The delivery still hurt after the
epidural?

CAROL
Um. Yeah. But hey, if it was really
so bad, I would have only had one
child.

ELEANOR
True. And you're kids are how far
apart?

CAROL
Four years. So I guess it took me a
bit to forget.

Carol laughs.

ELEANOR
Where are Adam and your beautiful
girls?

CAROL
Daddy and girls day. He took them
to the Bounce House. Rosaline
has a--

SOUND OF: doorbell.

ROSALINE
(remembering)
Richard!

Rosaline runs to her room.

ROSALINE (cont'd)
Tell him I'm not ready.

ELEANOR
Who's...

CAROL
A date.

ELEANOR
I see.

Carol opens the back door to the kitchen to see Richard.

CAROL

Hi, Richard, come on in. Rosie will
be a minute.

RICHARD

No problem. And I wanted to say
again, that this is not a date, I
just wanted to--

CAROL

Get Rosie among people. Yeah, Adam
did say that.

Eleanor snacks on some carrots in a Ziploc bag.

CAROL (cont'd)

Richard, this is Eleanor, she and
I used to work together.

RICHARD

Pleased to meet you. Richard.

ELEANOR

You didn't go to West High School,
did you?

RICHARD

No, why?

ELEANOR

Because you have manners.

RICHARD
(blushing)
Is that where you teach?

ELEANOR
(rubbing her belly)
Till this one is born.

RICHARD
Congratulations.

Rosaline rushes into the kitchen.

ROSALINE
Sorry to keep you waiting.

RICHARD
You know I don't mind waiting for
you.

ELEANOR
Awe.

CAROL
Richard, have her back by 9pm.

RICHARD
Roger that.

Rosaline gives her mom a kiss on the cheek goodbye.

ROSALINE
Thanks, mom.

As Richard and Rosaline exit the door.

ROSALINE (cont'd)
Have you ever thought of having a
baby?

The door closes.

Eleanor nearly chokes on her food. Carol and Eleanor share a glance as if to say, "oh no."

EXT. FARMER'S MARKET - ESTABLISHING - DAY

Rows of tents make up a local farmer's market of food, crafts, and art for sale.

EXT. FARMER'S MARKET - CONTINUOUS

Rosie and Richard are among the crowd. Rosie glances around at the crowd, a little nervous but soon warms up to interacting with people.

INT. PIZZA RESTURANT - LATER - DAY

Richard and Rosie sit at a corner table in a mom & pop pizza place. They look over the menus.

RICHARD
I found out more about Rosalind
Franklin. She's quite amazing, actually.
Because of her we know how genetic
information is passed from parents
to children.
(beat)
She was a strong women; she
suffered great hostility probably
just because she was a woman.

More interested in the menu...

ROSALINE
Humph.

                    RICHARD
          From what I can tell there was no
          real relationship between your Dr.
          Johnson and Franklin. He wrote her
          letters constantly, but we can't
          find any replies. He showed up at
          one of her talks in the states, but
          there is no record of them meeting.

Rosaline points to herself.

                RICHARD (cont'd)
          He must have got her DNA at some
                    point.

                    ROSALINE
          It's okay. I've decided that I'm
          just going to learn how to be me.

SOUND of Richard's cell phone.

                    RICHARD
                   (to Rosie)
          One second, okay?

Richard walks off to reveal Vincends, Big Man's assistant, standing
at the counter. Vincends holds a small glass of wine. He drops a
PILL into it and approaches Rosaline.

                    VINCENDS
                   (to Rosie)
          You look lonely.

                    ROSALINE
          No, he just stepped a-- he's coming
                    back.

                    VINCENDS
          Have you tried their wine? It's
          really good.

                    ROSALINE
             I've never had wine.

                    VINCENDS
             You should try it. You look
                    thirsty.

                    ROSALINE
             What does it taste like?

                    VINCENDS
             Grapes.

                    ROSALINE
             Okay.

Rosie takes a sip. Jerks back slightly.

                    VINCENDS
             It's got a bite to it.

                    ROSALINE
             I like it.

                    VINCENDS
             Can I sit?

INSERT - Big Man sits in the backseat of a car and watches
through the windows.

BACK TO SCENE

Richard returns.

                    RICHARD
             Hey, that seat's taken.

                    VINCENDS
             Oh, I'm sorry.

Rosie finishes her wine.

> RICHARD
> Don't act like I don't know
> who you are.

> VINCENDS
> I was just finishing up our
> conversation. Take care of her,
> will you?

Vincends pats Richard on the back as he leaves.

INT. CAR/BIG MAN'S - DAY - CONTINUOUS

Vincends enters the car.

> BIG MAN
> Is that her?

Vincends nods.

> BIG MAN (cont'd)
> She's a cute little thing. Small
> and feisty. I want her for the
> project.

INT. PIZZA RESTURANT - MOMENTS LATER - DAY

                    RICHARD
          What did that guy say to you?

                    ROSALINE
               (slightly drunk)
               Nothin'.

                    RICHARD
          I don't want you talking to him.

                    ROSALINE
               Okay.
               (changing subject
               abruptly)
          I thought of a question.

                    RICHARD
               Okay.

                    ROSALINE
          What do you want to be when you
               grow up?

                    RICHARD
               A detective.

                    ROSALINE
          Oh. And you are. You're so lucky.

                    RICHARD
               And you?

                    ROSALINE
          I wanna be a mommy.
               (bursting)
          A baby kicked me today!

Rosaline lifts up her shirt and rubs her belly.

ROSALINE (cont'd)
I'm trying to imagine what it would
be like to have a life growing
inside you. I mean it's weird,
right? But just imagine knowing
it's life you're nurturing and
creating.

RICHARD
(pointing to the wine glass)
Did he give you that?

ROSALINE
Why?

Richard points to the fact that Rosaline has her belly exposed.
Rosaline, embarrassed, pulls her shirt down.

ROSALINE (cont'd)
Sorry.

EXT. HOUSE BACK DOOR - NIGHT

Richard walks Rosaline to the door. Rosaline is drunk and
wobbling. Richard tries to hold her steady.

ROSALINE
I had a nice time. Sorry I'm woooo--

RICHARD
You're lovely.

ROSALINE
You're lovely.

RICHARD
You're also drunk.

ROSALINE
So, you never answered my question.

RICHARD
Which question was that?

ROSALINE
You silly, if you gonna help me get
a baby or not.

RICHARD
(nervous laughter)
I thought you were kidding.

ROSALINE
I'm not kidding. Kid, kidding, get
it.
(beat)
I like you.

RICHARD
I like you too.

ROSALINE
Kiss me like they do in the
magazines.

RICHARD
Um, I don't know.

ROSALINE
Richard, I've never been kissed
before.

RICHARD
I believe you.

ROSALINE
Please.

Richard pulls Rosie close to him.

RICHARD
Rose--

ROSALINE
I like when you call me Rose.

RICHARD
Rose, believe me when I say, I want
to see you again.

Richard leans forward and kisses Rosaline on the forehead.

With closed eyes, Rosie exhales.

RICHARD (cont'd)
Good night, Rose.

ROSALINE
Good night, Richard.

INT. KITCHEN - NIGHT - MOMENTS LATER

Rosaline enters the house and proclaims...

ROSALINE
I'm going to have Richard's baby!

INT. BATHROOM - NIGHT - MOMENTS LATER

Rosaline's head pukes in a toilet. She lifts her head to reveal Carol
sitting on the edge of the bathtub.

CAROL
Done?

Rosaline motions for one more time before puking again.

CAROL (cont'd)
How ya feelin' now?

Rosaline sits on the floor and leans against the wall in exhaustion.

                    ROSALINE
          Everything stopped spinning.

                     CAROL
          That's good.
                     (beat)
          You know, honey. I don't think
          you're ready to have a baby.

                    ROSALINE
          But I want to be.

                     CAROL
          Adam and I had a 5 year plan. We
          took those five years to learn
          about each other, grow with each
          other, and have fun before Mia and
          Lizzie entered the picture. You're
          still young, take the time, have a
          full life before you think about
                     kids.

                    ROSALINE
          But if creating life is something
          only a woman can do, I want to
          experience it so I can feel whole.

                     CAROL
          There is more to being a woman than
          birthing babies.

Rosaline squawfs.

                 CAROL (cont'd)
          We also have to consider if you can
          have kids.

                    ROSALINE
                 What do you mean?

                     CAROL
            I was determined to never use the
            "analog" word and teach you and
               treat you as human - as my
                   daughter. But--

                    ROSALINE
              I need to have more tests.

                     CAROL
                      Yup.

INT. WAITING ROOM/DOCTOR'S OFFICE - DAY

The Snooty Secretary from before hands Carol a medical file. With
COPY stamped in red over it.

                   SECRETARY
              Rune said you needed this.

                     CAROL
                   Thank you.

                   SECRETARY
              The doctor will see you both
                    momentary.

                     CAROL
                   Thank you.

INT. EXAM ROOM/DOCTOR'S OFFICE - DAY - MOMENTS
LATER

Rosaline sits on the exam table. Carol is reading Rosaline's file when
the DOCTOR enters.

DOCTOR
Rosaline? How are we today?

ROSALINE
Good I guess.

DOCTOR
We're going to follow up on the
tests we did last time. Some of the
procedures might be a bit more
invasive.

CAROL
More invasive? She was crying for
hours last time.

DOCTOR
We see what we can do, okay?

Doctor pulls up a small rolling stool and shimmies over to Rosaline.

DOCTOR (cont'd)
Do you have any concerns or
questions?

ROSALINE
I want to know if I can have a
baby.

DOCTOR
As I am sure you are fully aware of
your special situation, I don't
medically and scientifically advise
of pregnancy.

ROSALINE
But can I have a baby?

DOCTOR
No.

INT. WAITING ROOM/DOCTOR'S OFFICE -
CONTINUOUS

The empty waiting room echo's Rosaline's scream.

ROSALINE (V.O.)
NOOOOOOOOOOOOO!

INT. EXAM ROOM/DOCTOR'S OFFICE - CONTINUOUS

Carol hugs Rosaline who cries hysterically.

ROSALINE
It's not fair! It's not fair!

CAROL
I know, honey. Let it out.

ROSALINE
I just wanted to be a mom so bad.

CAROL
You still can be.

ROSALINE
But he's saying I can't have a
baby! He's saying I'm not a woman.

CAROL
He's not saying you're not a woman.

ROSALINE
Why can't I have a baby?! Why! Why!
Why!
(beat)
Why did he make me a woman if I
can't have a baby!

Carol hugs Rosaline closer.

Doctor exits the room.

INT. HALLWAY/HOSPITAL - CONTINUOUS

As the Doctor exits the room, he is approached by Vincends who whispers in his ear.

INT. KITCHEN - EVENING

Adam arrives home from work through the back door. Mia greets him.

                    MIA
                   Daddy!

                   ADAM
          There's my little princess.

              ADAM (cont'd)
            Where's Rosaline?

                  CAROL
         She's barricaded herself in the
                girls' room.

                   ADAM
          She had her tests today?

                  CAROL
                  Yeah.

                   ADAM
         What did they say about...?

Carol shakes her head "No."

              ADAM (cont'd)
                 I see.

MIA
Daddy, I made a new art project in
school, wanna see?

ADAM
Can it wait just a few minutes. I
want to check on Rosaline.

MIA
Daaa-ddy.

ADAM
I would love to see your project,
and I want to give it my full
attention. You can show me in a few
minutes. Okay? It's not going to
self-destruct, is it?

MIA
(laughing)
No, daddy, that's silly.

Adam rubs Mia and Lizzie's head and heads off to...

INT. DOOR/GIRLS ROOM - EVENING - CONTINUOUS

Adam opens the door a crack.

ADAM
Rosaline? Can I come in?

INT. GIRLS ROOM - EVENING - CONTINUOUS

Rosaline is huddled in a ball. She leans against the wall with her knees in her chest. She looks to the door and can see Adam though the crack.

                    ADAM
                    Please?

Rosaline removes the barricade of toys and let's Adam in.

                    ADAM (cont'd)
                    Pretty sad day, huh?

Rosaline nods.

                    ADAM (cont'd)
                    I know how it feels when a dream
                    dies.

                    ROSALINE
                    You do?

                    ADAM
                    When I was younger, I wanted to be a
                    baseball player, like Rickey
                    Henderson.

                    ROSALINE
                    Who?

                    ADAM
                    You don't know the Man of Steal?
                    Greatest leadoff hitter and base
                    runner? He holds the major league
                    records for career stolen bases,
                    runs scored, unintentional walks
                    and leadoff home runs. Played for
                    the Oakland A's, the Yankees, and
                    the Blue Jays...I wasn't the

strongest hitter so I wanted to
learn to steal bases like
Henderson. I would spend evenings
running up and down my parents long
driveway, timing myself, always
trying to get faster. Then one day
I was climbing trees with my
friends. We were razzing each other
who could reach the furthest. I was a
competitive rat back then
and I knew I could reach the
top...But I lost my footing and
fell...and broke my leg. I remember
crying and howling. My friends
thought it was the fact that my
bone was sticking out of my leg,
but really I was crying because I
knew my baseball dreams were over.
(beat)
Giving up on a dream was hard.
Harder than I think I have the
words to explain properly. But the
truth is breaking my leg was
probably the best thing that could
have happened.

ROSALINE
Really?

ADAM
I wouldn't have said that then. It
feels weird saying it now, but it's
true. If I didn't hurt my leg I
wouldn't have gotten into computer
technology. Wouldn't have met
Carol...There's a saying, when a
door closes, go out the window.
(beat)
Don't let anything stop you from
moving forward. It may not be the

dream you had planned but there is
another dream and another path
always waiting for you.

Rosaline scratches her arm. She has a band-aid in the bend of her
arm where an injection would be.

ROSALINE
Dad?

ADAM
Yes, Rosie?

ROSALINE
Thank you.

ADAM
Something wrong with your arm?

ROSALINE
I got a new shot today. It itches.

ADAM
Well, let me know if it gets worse,
okay?

ROSALINE
Okay, I'm sure it's fine...Dad?

ADAM
Yes, Rosie?

ROSALINE
I made a fool of myself in front of
Richard.

ADAM
I talked to Richard.

                    ROSALINE
                     When?

                      ADAM
            About thirty seconds after you came
             into the house screaming you were
                  going to have his baby.

                    ROSALINE
            Oops. Worried you, didn't I?

                      ADAM
               Little bit. Little bit.
                     (beat)
             Richard cares for you. In fact he's
                  waiting out front.

Rosie smiles.

                  ADAM (cont'd)
             But just take it slow, okay. I'm
           not ready for you to grow up, okay?

                    ROSALINE
                    Okay, dad.

They hug. Rosie exits.

INT. LIVING ROOM - EVENING

Richard stands in the living room. Rosie approaches.

                    RICHARD
             I brought another movie.

                    ROSALINE
                     Thanks.
                (thinking - scared)
           Is there dinosaurs in this one?

RICHARD
No. I promise there are no
dinosaurs in this one. I wouldn't
make that mistake again.

INT. LIVING ROOM - NIGHT

Rosaline has fallen asleep on Richard. Her face is tense and she's
flinching.

INT. EXAM ROOM/DOCTOR'S OFFICE - DREAM
SEQUENCE

Doctor holds a syringe.

DOCTOR
This will help your situation.

The needle goes into Rosaline's arm.

ROSALINE
It burns!

DOCTOR
I'm sorry.

SMASH CUT:

INT. LIVING ROOM - NIGHT - MOMENTS LATER

Rosaline wakes up suddenly. Her eyes have dark circles around them. She moves as if she's drugged. Rosaline shuffles to her feet.

> RICHARD
> Rose?
> (beat)
> Rose, you okay?

Rosaline stars to sway like she's going to fall down. Richard leaps for her. Rosaline falls into his arms and starts to SEIZE.

> RICHARD (cont'd)
> Rose! Wake up! Rose can you hear
> me? Stay with me. Stay with me.
> Don't you die on me.

At that moment,. Richard realizes how much he cares for Rosie.

INT. WAITING AREA HOSPITAL - MORNING

Carol, Adam, Lizzie, and Mia sit impatiently. Adam paces. Lizzie is on Carol's lap. Mia sits with her legs tucked into her stomach holding protector dragon. There is a suitcase nearby Carol.

> ADAM
> (to Carol)
> Has anyone talked to you?

Carol shakes her head "no."

> MIA
> How much longer?

> CAROL
> Patience.

> MIA
> I am but, I'm worried about her.

CAROL
I know, honey. We all are.

LIZZIE
Rosie, no like doctors.

CAROL
That's right, sweetie.

Richard approaches.

CAROL (cont'd)
(frantic)
Richard! What have they said? Do
they know what's wrong? When can we
see her? Do they know she's a--

RICHARD
She's in a coma but the doctor says
her vitals are good.

ADAM
Thanks for bringing her here.

CAROL
(near tears)
They said the shot was
routine. I should have never listen
to them.

ADAM
She's in good hands now.

CAROL
(to Richard)
I've packed Rosie's
things. The ACC knows too much
about us. The only way to keep her
safe is to get her as far away from

us as possible. Can you promise me
that you will take her far away?

RICHARD
But you're her family.

CAROL
And we will always be her family,
but we love her so much that we
have to let her go to save her.

Richard nods.

MIA
(to Richard)
Can you give Rosie protector
dragon?

RICHARD
I don't know.

MIA
I need my big sister to have it. It
will keep her safe until I can
see her again.

RICHARD
Roger that.

ADAM
Take good care of our Rosie, will
ya? Don't write or call directly.
Don't do anything that will put her
in jeopardy, okay?

RICHARD
Okay.

CAROL
Thank you.

The family hugs Richard as if they were hugging Rosie goodbye.

INT. LOBBY/HOSPITAL- CONTINUOUS - DAY

OVERHEAD SHOT of the family leaving the hospital lobby. We PULL BACK to reveal Rune watching them from the balcony.

INT. WAITING AREA/HOSPITAL - DAY -LATER

Richard sits with his head in his hands, tired/stressed. He looks up. Rune enters.

                    RUNE (O.S)
          Taking your job awfully personal,
                aren't you, detective?

                   RUNE (cont'd)
          Make no mistake, it will be coming
                     with us.

                    RICHARD
                    (defiant)
                 She has a name.

                     RUNE
             To me it has a number.

Richard lunges forward and grabs Rune by the shirt collar and pushes him to the wall.

                    RICHARD
              Just because you don't have a
             family you think you can destroy
                      others?
                     (beat)
             John Rune, decorated FBI agent,
              once a member of the president's
              motorcade. Had a bit of a drinking
             problem, did you? What happened to

your family?

Rune glares with anger and grief toward Richard.

RICHARD (cont'd)
You killed them, didn't you?

RUNE
It was an accident.

RICHARD
Drunk driving, right? Who was
drinking?

Rune shakes his head. He's not going to answer.

RICHARD (cont'd)
(forceful)
Who was driving?!

RUNE
(gritting his teeth)
You already know it was
me...detective.

RICHARD
You know what it's like to be

without your family.

                    RUNE
                It's too late.

                  RICHARD
              It's never too late.

                    RUNE
              It's too late for her.

EXT. FIELD (DREAM SEQUENCE) - DAY

Rosaline walks along a pier leading to the water.

At the end of the pier there is a FIGURE.
The figure turns around - It's her.

Rosalind and Rosaline approach each other.

                  ROSALIND
              What are you doing?

                  ROSALINE
      You gotta help me out here, I don't
            know what's going on--

                  ROSALIND
        Everything we've worked for is
              going to be ruined.

ROSALINE
I don't know what you mean.

ROSALIND
Wake up and see what you are doing.

ROSALINE
What? What am I doing?

ROSALIND
You're giving up.

ROSALINE
I'm not giving up.

ROSALIND
I don't believe you.

ROSALINE
What's to believe? I can't prove
it.

ROSALIND
Fight.

ROSALINE
Fight for what?

ROSALIND
For us.

ROSALINE
Us?

ROSALIND
For what you want most.

ROSALINE
Am I human?

ROSALIND
Is your heart still beating?

Rosaline puts her hand to feel her heart beat within her chest.

SOUND OF a heartbeat.

ROSALIND (cont'd)
How long has your heart beat in
your chest?

ROSALINE
Always.

ROSALIND
How long have you been human?

ROSALINE
Always.

ROSALIND
What makes us human? What makes our
heart beat?

SOUNDS of a heartbeat get louder and faster. Rosaline closes her
eyes. Rosaline opens her eyes.

ROSALINE
Love.

ROSALIND
You have people who love you.
That's a rare gift and never to be
discounted. It is the weaponry we
need to win the battle of life.
(beat)
Can you fight?

                    ROSALINE
                    (mousey)
                    Yes.

                    ROSALIND
                    (stern)
                  Can you fight?

                    ROSALINE
                   (confident)
                    Yes.

                    ROSALIND
          Prove it. Prove it not to others,
       but to yourself....If you can't hold
                  on - hold on.

INT. HOSPITAL ROOM- MORNING

Rosaline lies on the hospital bed. Her eyes open wide; she take a
gulp of air. She sits up in bed. Takes a beat. Looks around.

INT. HOSPITAL HALLWAY - MORNING

Rosaline scurries though the hall looking for something. She runs
into Big Man.
                    BIG MAN
          You have a very smart boyfriend. But
                now you come with me.

Big Man grabs Rosie.

                    ROSALINE
                    Richard!!!

INT. STAIRWELLHOSPITAL - DAY -LATER

Big Man stands at the top of the stairwell. He holds Rosie tight and
keeps the syringe to her neck. Richard and then Rune approach the
stairs with guns drawn.

BIG MAN
(to Richard)
I wouldn't do that if I were you.

CU of the syringe to Rosie's neck.

BIG MAN (cont'd)
Silly policeman always thinking he has
the upper hand. Tell me, how much will
it kill you when I make her a soldier?

RICHARD
Is that what's in that syringe?

BIG MAN
No this will kill her. You see if I can't
have her, no one will.
Rune you disappoint me.

ROSALINE
(to Richard)
Richard, where's my family? Tell me
that they are okay.

RICHARD
Don't worry about that right now.

BIG MAN
(to Rosie)
That's right because I am your family now.
Your family ran away like scared little mice.
They can't protect you but I can. I will care
for you. I will make you a General...and if you
are good little solider like I know you can
be...I will clone you a new family.

ROSALINE
But--

RUNE
(to Big Man)
Why didn't you clone my family?

BIG MAN
Rune, this is not the time.

RUNE
How many years did I do your dirty
work? And for what? You said you
would bring my family back. I've seen you
sign orders to clone murders, rapists and
thieves, but not one order to clone my little
girl. You destroyed so many
families in your wake and you can
even own up to your promise to me.

Rune points his gun toward Big Man. Big Man reaches for his gun.

Rosie gets feisty. She tries everything to get away from Big Man's grasp . She claws at his arm, uses her elbows to jab him in the stomach, and then stomps on his foot. The combination forces Big Man to DROP THE SYRINGE and let go of Rosie enough to then SLAP her across the face.

Rosie falls to the ground with the syringe nearby. Big Man picks her up by her hair. Big Man points his gun at Rune.

BIG MAN
Rune, you are no longer an asset to me.

Big Man SHOOTS Rune. Rune falls to the ground.

BIG MAN (cont'd)
(to Richard)
Don't worry, I'll take
good care of
her.

RICHARD
Over my dead body.

BIG MAN
Okay.

Big Man shoots Richard in the shoulder. Richard falls to the ground.

ROSALINE
NOOO!

BIG MAN
(leaning Rosie back)
Lend me your hand and we'll conquer
the world.

Rosie reveals the syringe and STABS Big Man in the chest.

Big Man falls to the ground.

Rosie walks and then crawls to Richard.

ROSALINE
(frantic)
Richard. Please be okay, please
don't leave me. Hold on. Hold on.

Rosie pulls Richard up to a seated position. His shoulder is bleeding but he's alive.

ROSALINE (cont'd)
You know all those books I read
were crap.

RICHARD
Why is that?

ROSALINE
None of them could teach me to what
it really feels to be in love.

RICHARD
Is that right?

ROSALINE
I love you, Richard.

RICHARD
I love you, Rosie.

They share that epic-action movie kiss.

FADE OUT.

FADE IN:

INT. TV SET

News magazine style, Reporter Lisa sits in a chair and address the
camera.

REPORTER LISA
The doors to the Alliance Clone
Corporation once open are now
chained and locked. After 60 years
of stealing scientific research and
making human analogs for study and
for war, the ACC is no longer. We
first broke the story to you two

years ago thanks to Rosie Ownes.
Rosie, herself an Analog by one of
the first scientists to work for
the ACC, was instrumental to
bringing down the organization. She
led a research committee that
proved environmental imprinting
over instinctual imprinting. The
Analogs early into ACC's New Army
breeding program were showing no
sign of born hostility. Rosie
proved that Analogs deserved basic
human rights and that they could
live side-by-side us and we'd never
be able to tell the difference.

Rosie sits in an interview chair.

                    ROSALINE
Humans have a highly developed
brain and are capable of abstract
reasoning, language, introspection
and problem solving, so do Analogs.
Our DNA may be constructed or
stolen but we are human and we all
struggle to find just what makes
us, us. We all are trying to find
our perfect place in the world.

INT. LIVING ROOM - NIGHT

Adam enters. He carries an old board game.

                    ADAM
Found it.

Carol turns off the TV.

                    CAROL
I thought we talked about this.

120

ADAM
(to Richard)
Time for one game?

RICHARD
I've got to get her home.

ADAM
Where is Rosie?

CAROL
Saying good night to the girls.

Rosaline enter the living room. She now has a PREGNANT
BELLY and holds Protector Dragon.

ROSALINE
Mia insisted I take Protector
Dragon back for
(hand on belly)
this little guy.

CAROL
That's sweet.

RICHARD
Can I get you anything, love?

ROSALINE
No,
(beat)
I'm perfect.

Camera pans back.

Crane shot of pull back on the door and up to the sky filled with
the audio of the family playing the game.

FADE TO BLACK

Production Stories

Protector Dragon

The green and purple stuffed animal dragon plays a small part on the set of *Ingénue* but make no mistake he is a real life saver.

Protector Dragon was a gift to Kami Leach (who plays Mia in the film) when she was a baby. When Kami struggled with nightmares Protector Dragon was placed in her crib and he took her nightmares away.

Years later Kami's Grandmother was suffering from colon cancer. Kami ask if she could lend Protector Dragon to be by Grandma's side as she went through surgery and recovery. Kami's Grandmother's surgery removed her cancer and was given a new lease on life.

Kami then lent Protector Dragon to her Grandfather during 5 bypasses to his heart. She was happy to see on each visit to the hospital her Grandfather doing better and with Protector Dragon by his side.

Word came that Kami's Great Grandmother was scheduled for heart surgery and Protector Dragon was again delivered and assured a speedy and healthy recovery.

The real magic in this little stuffed animal is that a child believes in helping others in their times of need.

Hot! Hot! Hot!

Ingénue was filmed June 21-July 8, 2011. This is not a normally hot time in Noblesville, Indiana, or so production thought.

Temps hit record highs of 115 degrees. Cast, crew and the camera were treated with ice packs, cold water, popsicles, and cold towels, anything that would keep them hydrated and cool from the sweltering sun.

Because of inconsistency for sound, the air conditioner unit was turned off bring the interior temps to 104 degrees. Many cast and crew members took their lunch outside where it was a nice 90 degrees.

On Day 4, the big protestor scene, there was little escape from shade. The tents production provided did little to help. We had two reports of heat exhaustion that day. One of the protestors escaped to her car with a strong urge to be sick. Remarkably, she finished the scene. Soon after, Kate Chaplin starting seeing spots and nearly passed out. Mike Williams took over the last few shots outside the courthouse. Kate continued to film for another 6 hours.

On Day 8, Melissa Chapman (who plays Carol) arrived on set with a mind-numbing headache. Most likely to the heat the day before. Luckily we were filming in the hospital with plenty of private places to lie down between scenes.

On Day 9, the pier scene with the two Rosie's, we actually knew it was going to be wicked hot. The National Weather Service put out a heat advisory. We knew we had to get in and get out. We spend about 2 hours in 105 degrees with no shade when Sarah (who plays Rosie) lost her ability to speak. The heat got her. We got what we needed and rushed her to air conditioning and put every ice pack we had on her.

Hidden Lyrics

Kate writes to music, a lot and sometimes a few song lyrics find their way into the dialogue. *Ingénue* has three hidden song lyrics in the film.

Dylan Cashbaugh (DP) caught on to this during filming and it quickly became a running guessing game of finding the hidden lyrics. He got 2 out of 3.

White Stripes "We Are Going To Be Friends" - the scene with Carol and Adam talking about teaching their girls how to be women. Carol says "Number, letters, learn to spell." Kate listened to this song a lot to get the cadency and child-like wonder of the younger characters in the film.

Killers, "All These Things That I've Done" - the scene with two Rosie's at the pier. Rosalind says "If you can't hold on, hold on." Kate had this song on heavy rotation when writing this scene and the lead up being taken by Big Man. She was especially drawn to the cadence of "I've got soul but I'm not a solider" as she knew it would speak to Rosie's awaking.

Mumford and Sons, "Awake My Soul" - the scene where Big Man is pulling Rosie back by her hair he says, "Lend me your hand and we'll conquer the world." It's a slight change from the original lyric. This scene was rewritten several times and in different locations. For the final pages she listened to "Awake My Soul" because she felt the beginning of the song was in Big Man's point of view and the later was in Rosie's point of view.

Also on Kate's *Ingénue* Playlist:

Coldplay - The Scientist
Peter Gabriel - Shaking the Tree
Killers - Human
Nina Simone - I Wish (I knew how it feels to be free)
Boomtown Rats - I Don't Like Mondays

Finding Superhero's
by Amy Pauszek

When I think of Superheroes, I think of an individual or group of extraordinary people who come together and unite to make a positive difference in the world. The making of *Ingénue* is a perfect example of how organization, loyalty, and the kindness to pay it forward brought some amazing Superheroes together.

Working with Kate Chaplin is always such an honor because she is a brilliant and passionate writer/director who loves what she does and her work shines! My role as a Producer was to find the funding and sponsors to help keep the production costs down.

When Kate showed me the original budget for craft services I knew I could save thousands of dollars by simply including our local community. My goal was to fill our 30 plus cast and crew members up every day with a well balanced, high protein and delicious hearty meal. I decided to contact my own Superhero Friends in the community and thus our journey began.

I am a firm believer that what you give you get back ten folds more. I put myself to a test and vowed to have all of the food donated by Indy's best restaurants, the best housing provided for the out of town actors and crew and any additional extra needs/supplies to make our film run smoothly and effectively. I had a mission and was so amazed and appreciative by the outreach and generosity from the wonderful communities of Noblesville, Fishers, Carmel, Avon, and Indianapolis.

127

Kate made a sponsorship book which gave the local community a chance to be a part of the film. We wanted this local Indie film and our community to unite together. We offered to put their logo on the back of crew t-shirt's, on the highly-trafficked Karmic Courage website and a special thanks listing in the ending credits of the film. We also invited the sponsors to be extras in the film and they took us up on the deal! I bet before long, Ol' Hollywood will be calling them and they will have a new job!

I started calling on contacts from previous PR/community events I have worked on and was overwhelmed by the generosity that followed. We had complete meals of delicious pork, turkey, fish, pastas, pizza, salads, bread sticks, along with huge cupcakes, cakes, desserts and tons of gourmet popcorn. (Thank you Greeks Pizza, Cook's Pizza, Olive Garden, Red Lobster, Noodles & Company, Silver Dollar Bar, G.T. South's, Milano Inn, Daylight Donuts, Encore Desserts and More, Freshly Frosted Cupcakes, Gigi's Cupcakes of Fishers, and Just Pop In!)

I will never forget the gratitude I felt coming on set and serving the very best food from local and national restaurants. I have to admit - I think every lunch and dinner served to the cast and crew made them all happy campers! The best thing, I know that transpired in return, was that our cast and crew members raved about the food and became loyal customers for life. I was proud that we cut costs.

I was also excited when Aveda Fredric's Institutes came on board and donated their complete full services. Every day we had 2 professional make-up/hair designers and 1 student - we called them our "Ninjas" on the sets. Any mention of being shinny or a hair out of place, they would pop out of nowhere and be on the case.

Thanks to CVS Managers Calvin Fields and Fred Billings (*Ingénue* Actor) of The Noblesville CVS for donating the extra necessities like paper towels, coffee, toiletries, and the most important, cases of water and sunscreen for our 106 degree scenes.

I am forever grateful for Cambria Suites, A Gold Star Award-Winning Hotel, who generously donated their beautiful suites and exceptional customer service to our out-of-town cast and crew. I was told some cast members did not want to go home after their stay that Supergirl Karen Bowers provided!

Thanks also to Sun King Brewery - you kept everyone 21 and over very happy!

We had an amazing Wrap Party at one of my favorite local owned bars Whiskey Business Sports Bar and Entertainment. Superhero owners Robin McCaslin, Mike Doran, and their fabulous staff decorated, catered, provided a DJ, and even allowed our own David Kemp to perform a few songs from the film. We had fun all night and partied with one another even though...we had a 7 am Call the next day at ... IU Health Hospital. Yes, we even had the hospital location secured down by my best friend and partner in crime, Dr. Angela Henrikson. What a beautiful hospital and yes, props used in the doctor's office scene was the real deal thanks to Angela's help and expertise! This location was perfect and we really appreciated the hospitals patience and help during the 3 day of filming!

I truly don't know what we would have done without all of our sponsors ... not to mention my personal friends who have local businesses and immediately jumped aboard. (Thanks MK, Tracy, Michele, Christina, Lori, and Rachel!)

It is obvious we asked and were given and blessed above and beyond! I had the best experience working on *Ingénue*. I not only got to meet some wonderful new Superhero Friends - I also had the opportunity to reconnect with some high school and college friends. Who knew after all these years I would end up working on a film with these "blasts from the pasts!"

In the end, I have to say - working with Kate Chaplin is always an honor and a pleasure. I consider Kate as my mentor - my Superhero partner in crime and a true female role model to all. I love having the role as her official Publicist and PR Rep... and I always will continue to be loyal and true to my favorite "Queen of The Indie Films!"

Thank you to all the sponsors, cast and crew who united as Superheroes and made *Ingénue!* You all were a big part of it and it shows you wear your "Capes" well.

Vicki Lastovich

My first day on set, everyone was so friendly and wanted to talk to me. I met Melissa Chapman (Carol). We were talking about Grandmas. Melissa told me that her mother was so excited to become a grandmother. Melissa, said, "When a woman becomes a grandma, she blossoms into a whole new person." A grandma with love, happiness, and pride. Melissa said she was allergic to cats and forgot to bring her allergy medicine. Kate looked in her kitchen cupboards, but she could not find any allergy-relief medication. Melissa left to go to her sister's house about 15 minutes away to get some Claritin.

Josh Leach, Kate Chaplin's husband, was a good man and let the cast and crew have free access into his home for 11 days. When Carol's husband, Adam, (Raymond Kester) was talking in front of the bedroom mirror while cleaning his ear with a Q-tip, this is what Josh would say and do. Definitely, this scene needed to be in the movie.

I had the best job. It was my job to pick up my granddaughter, Samantha Leach, (age 5) at her house and take her to my house so we could play. One time, she was sleeping when I arrived. I was surprised she could sleep with all the talking and activity going on adjacent to her room. When she woke up and started to get dressed, Mike Williams, Assistant Director, yelled with his loud, strong voice that everyone obeyed, "Quiet on the Set. This is a Take." Samantha leaned against her bed and stopped. She stood there with only one leg inside a pair of pants. She stood still and did not move a muscle. I was amazed at her balance. When Samantha finished dressing, she packed her large, red tote bag with toys and was ready to go to Grandma's.

One afternoon when Samantha and I were leaving, I noticed a huge crane in front of her house. I had parked down the street and turned around in a nearby driveway so I would not be caught on film.

On a movie set there are lots of cables and wires strung everywhere on the floor as they extend from room to room. I remember someone needed an extension cord. One was unplugged from a laptop. "Here you go."

There should be no background noise on a movie set. That includes a siren that goes off at 11:00 every Friday morning, the street sweeper, a car going by on the street, or a neighbor across the street mowing their lawn. I remember  someone went over there and asked if he could stop mowing for a while. The neighbor did shut off his lawn mower.

A fun moment on set was when they were filming a scene in the living room. Kate yelled, "CUT. I can hear cats." Someone went running upstairs to deal with the cat.

Kate's dog, Trinity, a Smooth Fox Terrier, behaved very well with the cast and crew going in and out of her house at all hours of the day and night.

The scene with Carol teaching the alphabet to Rosaline and Lizzie at the kitchen table, the "G" card Rosaline did not recognize was because the picture on the card did not look like a goat.

Kate's daughter, Kami Leach, (age 10) asked her, "Where should my eyes look?" It was a great question for an actress to ask. Kami learned all her lines quickly and also remembered what clothes she was wearing on each day. With the hot weather, Kami wanted to have her hair cut. Mommy said, "Not until after the movie."

Three makeup artists received class credits from Aveda for working on a movie set. Katie, Kenzie and Brin were called "The Makeup Ninjas" because whenever anyone said makeup, one of them would go running and be right there to take care of it. Katie made Samantha feel special when she braided Samantha's hair to look just like Rosaline. Thank you, Aveda, for bringing beauty and style to Ingénue. Thank you, Amy Pauszek, for bringing Aveda to Ingénue.

Sarah Moore (Rosaline) told me, "There was lots of sweat on that bedroom carpet. So much sweat!" The scene with the girls looking through the Sixteen magazine on the bedroom floor, Kate just said, "Tell me what you see." All the lines were ad-libbed.

Kate Chaplin visited Mayor John Ditslear's office to receive permission to film outside the Courthouse building In Noblesville, Indiana. Thank you, City of Noblesville.

It was 100 degrees outside when filming Ingénue. Kate experienced heat exhaustion in front of the Courthouse in downtown Noblesville. The cast and crew were there and took excellent care of her. Thank you.

CVS donated Karmic Courage Productions a gift card. Thank you for having the supplies we needed for Ingénue. All of your bottles of water were consumed on set and were very much appreciated! Thank you, CVS, for sponsoring Ingénue. Thank you, Amy Pauszek, for contacting CVS.

Gigi Cupcakes donated boxes of cupcakes for Ingénue. I thought it was cute because my mom's nickname in high school was Gigi. Thank you, GiGi Cupcakes. They WERE so good! Thank you, Amy.

Just Pop In donated snack bags of popcorn and also 4 huge containers of popcorn. Our movie set was now complete. Every movie needs popcorn! One of the containers of popcorn can be seen on the coffee table in one of the scenes of Ingénue. Thank you, Just Pop In. Thank you, Amy.

Ingénue cast and crew had a Red Lobster cuisine for lunch one day. Thank you for the great food! Everyone just raved about it! Thank you, Red Lobster! Thank you, Amy, for contacting Red Lobster.

Amy Pauszek arranged Karmic Courage Productions to film at her doctor's office at IU Heath West Hospital. Thank you, IU Heath West, for the use of your state-of-the-art facility! Thank you, Amy.

Craig Lemons (Rune) sat and talked to Mark and me about his acting job with Kelsey Grammar. Craig was then notified that his scene was up next. He stood up immediately and told us he was going to die. He walked over to the elevator and did the scene with Detective Richard. Afterwards, Craig stopped by to see us and started again right where he left off.

When Rosaline (Sarah Moore) was in the examination room at IU Medical Center West, there was a picture of Greg Spurgin on the wall. Greg is the father of Chris Spurgin (Detective Richard).

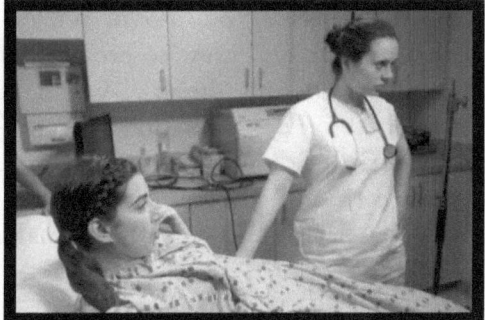

Mark and I sat in an examination room across the hall. We could hear Sarah's powerful screams radiating through the walls. They were loud and very convincing.

Bret Robinson, Still Photographer, walked into our room and noticed the skeleton figure on the window ledge did not have its jaw. He attached the jaw lying beside the skeleton. It must have been a jaw-dropping moment. While we were on set, so many of the crew members asked Mark and me if we would like some water. We were well taken care of. Amy told us we could help ourselves to anything in the refrigerator.

On the last few days of filming, Samantha said, "I want to be in a movie."

Whiskey Business hosted a great Wrap Party for Ingénue. They provided us a large buffet dinner and live entertainment. David Kemp was awesome! Thank you, Whiskey Business, for sponsoring Ingénue's Wrap Party and for sharing in our celebration of Ingénue. Thank you for all the great food! It was a fun and memorable evening for everyone! Thank you, Amy, for arranging Ingénue's Wrap Party with Whiskey Business. Thank you, Encore Desserts for the great cake. It was so beautiful and so delicious! Everyone enjoyed it!

Amy Pauszek, you have exceeded all of our expectations. Amy went over and beyond what we ever could have imagined. Amy is a Wonder Woman. Thank you for finding so many great sponsors to support Ingénue. "Amazing Amy," you have supplied us with Every One of our sponsors. Thank you for setting up the Indy Star and the radio interviews. Thank you for all you've done to promote Ingénue. "Amazing Amy" thank you for everything! Thanks again to all our sponsors for all your generous donations and contributions, your help and all your support to make Ingénue a huge success!

It was a fun movie set. Kate Chaplin worked with an excellent cast and crew to create Ingénue. It was great to see Kate Chaplin lead and direct. When Kate said, "ACTION," things happened. Everyone did a great job! Ingénue was absolutely fantastic! Congratulations Everyone! Kate, you are a great filmmaker; and the woman who knows how to get it done. Kate, you do what you do well. Keep making movies!

Melissa Chapman

I heard about auditions for *Ingénue* through Mid America Filmmakers. I had recently wrapped on an independent film where I had a negative experience and wasn't sure if I wanted to audition. I asked my friend Jessica Stone about Kate Chaplin. She could not speak highly enough of Kate: her professionalism, her style, her creativity, her personality, her previous film work and on and on. So, I auditioned for Kate in April. I liked her immediately and was thrilled when she called to offer me the role of Carol.

I loved the script when I read it and was excited to be a part of it! There are not a lot of movies that have good, solid, character roles for females. *Ingénue* did. The role of Carol was exciting for me because of the dynamic of her character. She was strong but fallible, smart but confused, loving but guarded. I enjoyed her journey and growth.

The entire cast and crew were phenomenal! Everyone did their job and did it well. When the temperature inside the house rose to 103 degrees, we all shared time at the fan, sweating and laughing together. I made some wonderful friendships with many of the cast and crew and still keep in touch (and always plan to)!

Kate was everything my friend Jessica said and more. I was very impressed with her. She runs a tight, professional, fun, supportive set. Everything I could need was provided. Kate was very approachable about her script, the wording, the emotion, everything. I had two serious emotional scenes and Kate was incredibly supportive. She gave me the freedom and encouragement to really give them all I had. She gave me much needed hugs after the scenes too!

Ingénue was a great experience! I am so thankful that I am part of it. I hope to work with Kate again!

Sarah Moore

Kate has three lovely pets (a dog and two cats). They like me. A lot.

I had to be very emotional in this film and the animals wanted desperately to comfort me. During a scene where I'm crying hysterically, Vinnie the incredibly old cat, came wandering into the shot, stopped right in front of me, sat down, and gave a plaintive meow. "Don't cry!" he seemed to say. "I love you!" Then he rubbed on my leg.

Trinity is a tiny terrier. She weighs about 8 pounds. During a pivotal scene in the film, I have a seizure. My co-star, Chris Spurgin, holds me down during the seizure and yells a lot. Trinity thought he was hurting me. She decided to save me from the big loud scary man. Trinity came rushing in and tried to drag me away by my leg. I weigh more than

8 pounds. It didn't work and I had bruises on my legs for a week from her teeth.

At least they were motivated to attack me with love.

Glenna Reinhardt

In 2012, I was lucky enough to be cast in the Kate Chaplain film *Ingénue*. I had worked with Kate before on a few other films, and when I found out she was doing a feature film, I couldn't audition fast enough! Even though it was the hottest summer in Indiana's history, filming was a lot of fun. Everyone worked together like a well oiled machine. It was a wonderful experience for me, and I am glad I got to be a part of it!

Craig Lemons

Having seen a couple short films by Karmic Courage Productions, I was excited to audition for a role in *Ingénue*. I prepared a monologue and set out for Noblesville, IN. The character of Rune kinda drew toward me, as much as I was drawn to it. I pride myself as an actor that plays characters that are a little out of the ordinary. Sinister and/or creepy seems to come natural to me. I'm a big fan of suspense, sci-fi, thriller films. *Ingénue* has these qualities and still has a great story of love to share. The entire cast and crew treated me exceptionally well. I got to work with some people again and I met some new friends for life. My *Ingénue* experience was one of the greatest highlights of my career to date.

Raymond Kester

When Kate first put out the audition notice for *Ingénue*, and I saw what the story was about, I knew that it was a project I wanted to be a part of. I was originally drawn by the science fiction element of the story, but was happily surprised by how good the characters and the relationships were. Once production got started and we started working together as a team, we all started to realize that we had a really good story about love and family. It was a different way to look at how an adoption changes and enhances the life of not only the adopted but those who bring a new member into their family. Shooting this film was a great experience. As a group of actors, technicians and production crew led by our hard-working director, we laughed and cried together and came to depend on each other. Made some great new friends and became closer to some old friends as well.

If I could change anything about the shoot of this film it would be the crazy heat we experienced during shooting. The first day, shooting in the basement, not so bad, but as we moved up into the other interior shots in the house, which had to have the air conditioner turned off for sound, the temperature began to rise and rise until the makeup crew had to re-apply powder almost between every shot so that we didn't appear as if we were in a steam room. The peak of this came when Sarah and I were shooting one of my favorite scenes in the film. It was a very soft tender moment where Adam really becomes a father to Rose, and as I was finishing the monologue, I could feel the sweat building up on my nose and getting to the point where it was going to bead up and drip off of my nose, but I think I was saved on that take because a truck or something drove by loudly and killed the sound. Makeup swooped in and took care of my shiny nose and we got the scene done.

Another first for this film for me is that both of my sons were able to be a part of it as well.

Larry E. Jones Jr.

I've known Kate for a few years through Indiana Filmmakers Network meetings. I was impressed by the stories, previous movies and success Kate had received. I always wanted to work with Kate on a project, but timing never seemed to fall into place. When I heard about *Ingénue* having auditions and the shoot schedule fell between two other projects, so I wrote a new monologue based on what I envisioned as a speech from Spartacus to the rebel slaves. I auditioned and was cast as Policeman #1. The time on the set was great and very professional. I truly enjoyed working with everyone involved in my scenes.

Simona Ciarlo

Being on the set of *Ingénue* was a wonderful experience. When I first arrived I thought it was a family production. Everyone was so close, friendly, and helpful. As I met those on set, one by one, I learned some had just met during the filming. Everyone got along so well.

Kate Chaplin directed with passion, and smile on her face. She wanted her actors to be comfortable, but she also wanted the story to come to life. She was thorough and consistent when it came to direction. I really admired her ability to let the actors be in a fun environment, yet pull them back graciously when it was time to film.

Playing Officer #2, I worked with Sarah Moore, Larry E. Jones, and Chris Spurgin. I even met up with Craig Lemons, who I'd only communicated with through Facebook, and whose IMBD page is growing rapidly! Sarah Moore was hilarious! She is so witty and the banter between her and Chris Spurgin kept me laughing between shoots.

Going into acting to rise above being shy and naturally quiet, the actors and crew made me feel at ease. Even the girls who did my hair and makeup were so personable. Being in only one scene, I wish I had more time to have spent with everyone and get to know them better. I'm thankful to have been able to be a part of *Ingénue*. I want to thank Kate Chaplin and Karmic Courage Productions for including me.

Koko Hart

My roommate introduced me to Dylan because he needed an AC for *Ingénue* and a place to crash in Indy. After the first weekend of shooting, we were quite interested in each other. And after *Ingénue* was said and done, Dylan continued staying at my place. Now, 6 months after *Ingénue*, we're still together!

Kylee Wall

As a member of the post production team (specifically, the visual effects and titling artist), I wasn't on *Ingénue's* set at all.

Except for that one afternoon I was.

If you know anything about this film's production, you already know it was shot during record-setting heat. If you don't already know this, let me explain this heat: IT WAS HOT. Humid, cloudless, dry, and boiling. This isn't movie diva whining, it was over 100 degrees most days. I believe my phone told me it was about 105 degrees Fahrenheit -- that is, right before it shut itself down with a heat warning.

I popped by the set in a small park where the scene was being set to shoot Rosie on a pier. One of the film's few VFX shots was taking place out here, and I was stopping by to make sure it was being shot the way I liked so I could composite it correctly. The shot happily came out perfectly, but it wasn't without dramatic loss in body fluids. It was the kind of heat that makes you beef jerky in an hour flat.

I stood by as the scene was scouted and everyone tried their hardest to stay in the shade. But the perfect spot for this exchange between Rosie and Rosie wasn't even close to the tiniest speck of shade, and the effort required to walk to the nearest spot was just too much.

It was the kind of heat you'd expect in the middle of the desert with vultures circling you overhead. I swear I saw a mirage or two out there.

In between takes, we drank lots of water and used the ice to try to keep Sarah's body temperature to a manageable state without wrecking her delicately crafted hair and makeup. Some ice was applied to some interesting areas. Sunscreen was applied and reapplied. Production assistants bought more water, more ice. Everything ran smoothly.

Which is impressive because it was the kind of heat that makes a person lose their mind or their temper. Or both.

I was only on the set for about three hours, but in that time I got a healthy dose of *Ingénue*. Many familiar faces on the set, a few new ones, and some impressive Midwestern talent that can run a tight set, even when they're melting.

A few hours later, I discovered the tops of my feet were burned with a clear outline of my flip lops. I shouldn't wear flip flops on a set anyway. Silly.

And even though it was the kind of heat that left you dried out and delirious in an hour tops, a movie got finished on time and on budget. And as I cranked up the AC in my edit cave to review the rushes for my VFX shots, I might have been fooled that it was shot on a balmy spring day.

Rosie Hoistion

My *Ingénue* adventure began one sunny day while working at a local, downtown Noblesville bookstore. My coworker called last minute and asked me to work for her; I was not even scheduled to work the day when Amy came in looking for local sponsors! Well being the superstar want-a-be that makes me Rosie, I pulled out pictures of my four year old grandson and told Ms. Amy we should be in the movies! Sadly my little man did not move to Noblesville until filming was done, but lucky me, I got to be an extra in the protest scene of *Ingénue*!! When I am old and gray, in my rocking chair, I will be able to tell everyone that listens to my silliness that I was in Kate Chaplin's first full length movie, *Ingénue*. Thank you Amy and Kate for making me a SuperStar!!!

Joshua Wooten

What was my experience on the set... well I was the Unit Production Manager. My job functions included building a preliminary budget, handling press releases and a million other things. My story started months before we shot one frame. I had worked with Kate on a previous project, *Love Dance* and wanted the opportunity to work with her again. I begged, pleated, cried, and asked a million times. Kate graciously allowed me on board. Then I hit the ground running. I built the budget based off Kate's framework and I sent lots of emails and productions assistance. During filming, I worked in the production office made sure releases were signed and made sure we were eating on time and everyone was working well together. Would I do it again? Yes.

Mark P. Jackson

The audition for *Ingénue* required that I do a monologue. I absolutely hate monologues and would much rather read dialogue from a script. I kind of scrambled around to find something for the audition. I came across a monologue called "I Hate Hamlet." It so happens that the characters' hatred for Hamlet kind of matched my hatred for monologues. I had found my monologue and it must have presented well to Kate because I got the roll of a bad guy in the film.

Cambria Suites

The Cambria Suites Hotel ~ Noblesville was proud to support Kate Chaplin and Karmic Courage Productions by hosting the actors at the hotel during the filming of *Ingénue*. I truly believe that as a member of the community it is our responsibility to help our local organizations and business achieve success. For without our local business and loyal guests, we would not be successful in our own ventures. Kate Chaplin showcased so many wonderful aspects of our community and did an amazing job promoting her vendors that supported her. Best of all- she was amazing to work with, her and her staff are hard working, professional and hilarious. I had a blast during our photo shot/ interview at the hotel.

Luke Broyles

It was so kind of Miss Kate to welcome me to the set; she was really cool and relaxed.

Terry Shepard

My *Ingénue* experience as best I can recall after the spending the afternoon in the blistering hot Indiana sun wearing a baby blue polyester sports jacket and contrasting bright pink Oxford. My friend and mentor, Kate, asked if I'd like a cameo in her first feature film. I read the script and instantly fell in love with the story. She was kind enough to cast me as a news reporter and allow me to revive a role from a story I wrote a year previous and she produced and directed. I remember waiting outside the Noblesville City Hall on that smoldering Sunday afternoon. We shot in between the AC unit's breaks from cooling the empty building. Chuck, the sound guy, would listen attentively, and then give us the go ahead during those short intervals. I also got to see my son, Jake, play an angry protester. It was great to share that experience and to be around a fantastic group of talented and amazing individuals. I am anxiously awaiting the debut of this film so I can show my friends and family that films can be made with positive, uplifting and all the while entertaining stories. These films can also be made right in the heartland and move and inspire just as much as any made a thousand miles away in Hollywood.

Mary Kay and Rosario Valenti

My son, Rosario and I were more than excited to be part of the feature film *Ingénue*. We travelled from Chicago, IL to be extras in the park scene. We stayed at the Cambria Suites in Noblesville and made a short vacation out of the experience. Amy Pauszek is one of my dearest friends and she brought this feature film to my attention. I was moved to have my company sponsor the film after reviewing some of Karmic Courage/Kate Chaplin's work. It's motivating to see women taking on lead positions in the industry and I wanted to support her endeavors. For my company it was great exposure and I appreciated being on the T-shirts and included in many materials associated with the film. On the set we experienced a very hot day but everyone was making the best of the conditions. They made sure the kids were hydrated and there were plenty of eats and treats for everyone to enjoy. Rosario really enjoyed the mysterious bug that showed up to be part of the cast. In my opinion, I think it was looking for the snack tent. It was filled with local goodies from sponsors of the film. It all made for some great moments and pictures. Our time on the set was brief but enjoyable. We made friends, shared many laughs and made some incredible memories. I was honored to have received an IMDB page for both Rosario and I. It was a delight to work with Kate, her staff and cast. After shooting, Rosario and I enjoyed the weekend in Indianapolis. Rosario has talked about our "Indy trip," many times and it always brings a smile to my face. Thank you for the experience and memories. I hope to work with you again in the future.

Lori Calwell Hopkins

Some might snicker at the idea of divine destiny but my daughter Rachel and I would disagree. Rachel had just finished her freshmen year at Ball State University, my alma mater. Rachel is studying Telecommunications with a major interest in film and I am a High School Theatre Arts, Speech, and English Teacher. My sister Terri has returned to college, and is interested in the performing arts and writing. The three of us had loosely formed a production company, TriFekta Productions, and are in the process of building. We had prayed for some performing arts opportunities and then went about our summer business of trying to find Rachel a job for both summer and the upcoming school year. Rachel and I went to Ball State on the first Friday in June to look for potential jobs for the following year.

This is where the divine enters. We decided to eat at Greeks Pizzeria in the village. It was a slow day, but from the time we approached and entered the building, there was a woman sitting in front of the window with a great deal of paperwork spread over the table who attracted my attention. With her fierce blue eyes and dark hair, she looked so familiar, I was sure I knew her. After we ate, we approached her table, and I asked her if she had gone to Ball State. As we talked, we realized that not only had she and I gone to Ball State at the same time, we had lived in the same residence hall, and had been friends while on campus. When she said her name was Amy Pauszek, a flood of memories regarding our Wood Hall days came back. Imagine our excitement when she told us about a movie project she was working on called *Ingénue* that was being filmed in Noblesville! She invited us to be extras and that was the beginning of a divine destiny and reconnection that I have been so blessed to experience.

Once we arrived on the set, my daughter Rachel said she recognized the director, Kate Chaplin, from a Hugh O'Brian Leadership Conference she had attended at Butler University during her sophomore year of high school. Rachel remembered Kate speaking about her independent filmmaking experiences out of the Indianapolis area. At the time, this sparked a new interest for Rachel in the possibility of something more from Indiana than corn. That experience fueled her interest in film and was one of the reasons she chose to pursue Telecommunications.

Being on the set of *Ingénue* only affirmed that quest for Rachel and reinforced the idea to continue developing good scripts and creative projects for my sister and I. Thanks for the GREAT opportunity!!!!

David Kemp

I was drawn to the guitar from an early age. I just loved all the sounds you could make. How expressive it is. When I was 9 or 10 my Grandma gave me my Uncle's old Harmony electric and Peavey amp. I wasn't serious about playing it yet but liked to plug it in and drum on the strings with pencils or toys, just making cool noise. By 12 I would straps it on and put on a tape and pretend I was Eddie Van Halen, Jimi Hendrix, Slash, or Ted Nugent. So at 13 I decided to get serious. My Dad taught me some chords and how to play "For What It's Worth" by Buffalo Springfield and "Paranoid" by Black Sabbath. He has been in bands since 1968. He is an amazing singer, songwriter, and bass player. We currently front the band Lowdown, a high octane blues/rock trio, together. In high school I joined jazz band. We were good; we won many competitions. I lettered both years I was there and won a soloist award.

Mainly I have been in bar bands, only recently getting into the film game. The short film *Love Dance* was the first time ever contributing to a movie. It is so awesome having the chance to score a feature film. *Ingénue* also marks my "acting" debut; Kate was gracious enough to allow me to be "Security Guard #1". It was so cool seeing how it all works. Typically a musician writes a song then practices it, records it, and then performs it live. What I saw that day was that entire process happening at the same time. It was freaking amazing. For this soundtrack I am using all of my resources, from my collection of guitars and effects to my Dad to my best friend, Eliese Davis (great singer/guitarist) to my wonderful wife, Melissa (who is a giant wealth of lyrics). Modern technology is amazing. For these tunes I was able to obtain a fantastic guitar processor. I was able to write and record full string sections or piano just by playing chords on the guitar. There my secret is out! HA-HA! I am so grateful for this opportunity and I cannot wait for the next one.

Barbara Clouse

I heard about this production from a friend from high school, Amy Pauszek. She asked if my daughter and I would like to be a protester in the movie! My daughter has been getting into acting in plays at school and at Young Actors Theatre so I said, "Yes!"

That day was hot! We met early at the courthouse and waited to see what to do! All of the other protestors were very nice. We made our own signs and brought them with us. Protesting is hard work! We had to yell and be angry and remember our places for several takes! It was very fun! Thank you to the cast and crew for putting up with a few rookies.

Liz Collar

I had an incredible experience working on the set of *Ingénue*. Everyone was so kind, thoughtful, hard working and positive all day. You know it's a great production when you can show up to film in the morning and make great friends by the end of the day!

Chris Spurgin

Working on a movie is a fun, amazing, and highly unpredictable experience. I've been doing it for probably close to ten years now, and no matter how well prepared everyone is, you still never know what might happen.

The first day I was on set was a long, hot day. We had been shooting for a while, and we came to a scene where I was to go charging out of the front door, chasing after someone. Now, this seems fairly uncomplicated when you think about it, but it is a little more delicate than you might imagine. The challenges I faced in pulling off this seemingly simple maneuver were twofold. To begin with, in order to pick up a little momentum, I had to give myself a few steps in the room. I wanted it to be convincing when I came bursting out! The problem was that the floor was entangled with a carpet of wires snaking this way and that. Part of the movie magic is that you never see all those cables, but, believe me, they're there. So just making it across the room without doing a face plant was my first problem, and it's not like I could be looking down while I was charging at the door. The camera might see that, which leads me to the second problem. The door I was going through is one of those outer doors, like a screen door, that has the glass in the upper part of it. It has one of those handle doorknobs, so it's more of an "L" shape rather than a knob. I didn't want to destroy the door by hitting it too hard, but I also wanted to hit it hard enough to sell the shot. Oh, and did I mention that I wasn't supposed to actually look at the door handle when I grabbed it? That's right, the camera sees that! So here I am, traversing a floor coiled with cords at speed and slamming through a door (but not TOO hard), all while keeping my eyes forward. You can probably guess what happened. On about the second or third take, after successfully making it across the floor, I made a grab for the knob, totally missed it, and I smacked my face right into the glass. I swear, my face print was left there for weeks, which I'm sure was totally by accident.

If you ever consider going into film, just remember, it doesn't always go as planned. Whether you're pressing your face into a glass door or you're introducing your character by the wrong name (yeah, I did that too), part of what makes it all so much fun is you just never know what's going to happen.

Elizabeth Hamilton-Guarino

I am so thankful for my book, *Pinky Doodle Bug* being in the movie *Ingénue*. I've known Amy Pauszek for many years now and I jumped at the chance to be included in this project. Amy is what I call a "dot connector." Amy sees chances to help promote her friends, their lives and interests. She emailed me and told me about the movie and said they needed a children's book to feature throughout. It was beautiful timing, as my book *Pinky Doodle Bug* had just been published and had just won a Mom's Choice Award and was featured at the Maine Festival of the Book in 2012.

With beautiful colorful illustrations by Maine's own Sandra Waugh, we hope *Pinky Doodle Bug* adds to Kate and Amy's vision of lighting up the world with their movies. Thank you. We feel blessed and honored for *Pinky Doodle Bug* to in the movie *Ingénue*.

Michele Shetter

My dear friend, Amy Pauszek, shared with me an opportunity for my boys and I to participate in a film shoot as an extra for a protest scene. I've never met anyone that can say no to Amy! Knowing nothing really about the film my two teenage sons, Nathan and Josh showed up one August morning bright and early to a parking lot in Noblesville to protest cloning. We had no idea what we were getting into.

We had a total blast! From the moment we arrived at the parking lot and got out of our car we were greeted by chipper Amy and was made to feel welcome immediately. We followed the crowd of people that had arrived and were given instructions about our valuable role in the production. The Mike Williams (AD) was hilarious and my boys and I knew immediately we were going to really get "into" our part! Watching all the behind the scenes work was so fascinating and thrilling to observe. Everyone on staff was so professional and very respectful to us volunteers. The director herself was so fun to watch because of her vision, creativity and was calm, cool and collected as she worked with everyone. Kate, the director, made all of us feel so welcome and special for being a part of her film. When they announced action, my boys and I were competing with each other to see who could be more outraged with the thought of cloning. (That was our task in the film). Every time they stopped the scene my sons and I would laugh so much with each other and would argue as to which one of us was more into our part. We were actually bummed when they told us our participation was complete because we were having an absolute blast trying to one up each other and be the best actor there! Thank you Kate and Amy for letting my sons and I participate in your film.

Jake Shepard

I had worked with Kate before as a PA on a previous film and it was a surprisingly enjoyable experience, so when I was told that she was looking for some extras for a film, a full feature no less, I was eager to help out and do my first bit of acting. The job was close to what one could assume an extra role to be, a nice bit of fun in a scene with multiple parts, which of course can make for a bit of tedium. You'll find me in a group of protesters holding a sign that says "God Hates Clones" (an issue I've never really had an opinion on) while making myself as loud and as emotion-driven as I possibly could. (Two things I rarely do, if at all) Still, even introverts who prefer to work behind the scenes can have a lot of fun making fools of themselves in movies, especially when the main characters are anything but. It was an interesting time, that's for sure, and even though I liked PA work better, it's an experience I'd gladly have again.

cast and crew credits

KARMIC COURAGE PRODUCTIONS
in association with VIMAR
presents
a Kate Chaplin film

INGENUE

Music by	Written/Directed By	Edited by
David Kemp	Kate Chaplin	Katie Toomey
Director of	Produced by	Visual Effects by
Photography by	Kate Chaplin	Kylee Wall
Dylan Cashbaugh	Mark Lastovich	
	Vicki Lastovich	
	Amy Pauszek	

CAST IN ORDER OF APPEARANCE

Adam	Raymond Kester
Carol	Melissa Chapman
Mia	Kami Leach
Lizzie	Jamie Angel
Rosaline	Sarah Moore
Police Officer #1	Larry E. Jones Jr.
Police Officer #2	Simona Ciarlo
Detective Richard	Chris Spurgin
Big Man	Tristan Ross
Vincends	Mark P. Jackson

John Rune	Craig Lemons
Dog	Trinity
April	Liz Collar
Alex	Wyatt Kester
Olderboy	Dawson Kester
Playground Kids	Rosario Valenti
	Samantha Leach
	Jensen Moore
	Abby Line
Playground Moms	Mary Kay Valenti
	Amy Beers
	Stephanie Lynn
	Tracy Line
Cold Doctor	Dave Butts
Cold Nurse	Ellie Bradford
Mean Secretary	Amy Pauszek
Guard #1	David Kemp
Guard #2	Scott Russell
Sophia	Indigo Moore
Protestors	Mathew W. Allen
	Sandy Rusk
	Richard Hackel
	Lori Caldwell Hopkins
	Rachel Jean Hopkins
	Kylie Clouse
	Raniya Naizi
	Noah Billings
	Michele Shetter
	Barbara Clouse
	Alan Simpson
	Christina Hubbard
	Faith Billings
	Josh Shetter
	Nate Shetter
	Sara Niazi
	Ryaan Niazi
	Fred Billings
	Cindy Simpson
	Rose Kelley Hoistion
	Shelley Kornman
	Alex Morse
	Terri Butler
	Jake Shepard

Reporter Lisa	Glenna Reinhardt
Reporter #2	Terry Shepard
Berg Johnson	David Ross
Eleanor	Gina Moffett
Baby at Market	Jonah Harris
Mom at Market	Katie Harris
Doctor Reese	Jeff Angel

CREW

Unit Production Manager	Joshua Wooten
1st Assistant Director	Michael Williams
2nd Assistant Director	Riley Vickery
First Assistant Camera	Caz Tanner
Second Asst. Camera	Koko Hart
Grip	Angela Sorury
	Bret Robinson
Dolly/Crane/Grip	Eric Ridge
	Bret Robinson
	Dakota Hart
	Corey Boschet
	Nathan Issacs
	Riley Vickrey
	Michael Williams
	Joshua Wooten
	Paul Zink
Gaffer	Austin Gardner
Still Photographer	Bret Robinson
	Jennifer Spurgin
Sound Mixer	Chuck Budreau
	Nathan Issacs
Boom Operator	Corey Boschet
	Nathan Issacs
Costumer	Glenna Reinhardt
Set Designer	Valerie Pearce
Storyboard Artist	Kate Chaplin
Script Supervisor	David J. Syzcylo
Make Up/Hair	Katherine Vance Hammonds
	MaKenzi Presnell
	Briana Youn
Production Assistant	Luke Broyles
	Kathie Green
	Tammy Legere

	Troy Maynard
	Paul Zink
Stunt Coordinator	Dylan Cashbaugh
Stunt Driver	Joshua Wooten
Unit Publicist	Amy Pauszek

Sound Editor	Maura Sherrer
Title Design	Kylee Wall
Visual Effects by	Kylee Wall
Color Correction	Katie Toomey

SUPPLIES

Make up	Aveda Fredric's Institute
Crane	Eric Ridge
Prop Guns	BGB Productions
	Daniel Head
Medical Office	Angela M.D.
Lighting	Bret Robinson
Sound Equipment	Chuck Budreau
Sound Effect	www.freefx.co.uk
Meals Provided by	Milano Inn
	Noodles & Company, Noblesville
	Encore Desserts & More
	Red Lobster, Avon
	Olive Garden, Noblesville
	Olive Garden, Avon
	Greeks Pizza, Noblesville
	Silver Dollar Bar & Grill
	Gigi's Cupcakes
	Just Pop In
	Daylight Donuts
	Cooks Pizza
	Sun King Brewing Company
	G.T. Souths
Wrap Party	Whiskey Business Sports Bar and Entertainment
Accommodations	Cambria Suites

SONGS

"Just One Minute More"	"Papercup Romance"
Written by William Kemp Jr	Written by Eliese Davie
Performed by William Kemp Jr	Performed by Eliese David
Recorded by Pete Brown	Recorded by David Kemp

"Giant Man"
Written by William Kemp Jr
Performed and Recorded by
David Kemp

"God Hates Clones"
Written by David Kemp
Performed by Lowdown
Recorded by David Kemp

"Nonplus"
Written by Melissa and
David Kemp
Performed by Deadbeat Heroes
Recorded by David Kemp

"ACGT"
"Dream"
"Dog Tale"
"Showdown"
Written, Performed,
Recorded by David Kemp

"Broken Again"
Written by David and
William Kemp Jr.
Performed by Lowdown
Recorded by David Kemp

'Hypothesis"
Written by Eliese Davis,
Melissa and David Kemp
Performed by Deadbeat Heroes
Recorded by David Kemp

"Cucumber Cool"
Written by Melissa Kemp and
David Kemp
Performed by Lowdown
Featuring Eliese Davis]
Recorded by David Kemp

"Unlight"
"Final Count"
"Comfortable Mystery 2"
"Perif"
"Zombie Hoodoo"
by Kevin MacLeod
(incompetech.com)
Licensed under Creative
Commons by Attribution 3.0

Special Thanks to:
Mark Lastovich, Vicki Lastovich, Amy Pauszek, City of Noblesville, Diane Kagel, Bretorious Photography, Noblesville Travel, CVS - Hamilton Town Center, Village Dental, Michele's Studio, Angela Henriksen, Days & Knights, Reel Hope Film Festival, Luke Productions LLC, Jiffy Lube Beech Grove, Freshly Frosted, Anonymous Jumbo Scrimp Records, K&L Cards, Larry Jones Jr, Today's Furniture and Mattress, M.K. Valenti, Try Fekta Productions, Best Ever You, Pinky Doodle Bug, Jennifer Parker Pictures, Claudia Smiles, Craig Lemons, Mary Houghton, Glenna Reinhardt, Jeff Curry, Bret Robinson, Katie Harris, Troy Maynard, Chuck Budreau, Ron Apple, Katie Toomey, Kylee Wall, Apple

Ardent Scott, Elijah Williamson-Jones, Kerra Wagner, Catherine Crouch, Peter Hackman, Simona Ciarlo, Lynn Budreau, Terry Sheppard, Joshua Wooten, Krystle Lastovich, Dan Lastovich, Brandon Darney, Jessica Stone, Casey Ryan Stone, Loi Caldwell-Hopkins, Chis Spurgin, Bill Fouts, T.J. Banes, Kevin Elliott, Calvin Fields, Diane Palumbo, Karen Bowers, Jeremy Geisendorff, Robin McCaslin, Mike Doran, Frederic J. Holzberger, Sarah Hoback, Kurt Kulhavy, Sandy on the Scene, Indy Film News, Do it Indy, Gamer Chick, Starbase Indy, Spin Texas, Sticker Banners, DCG Graphics

Filmed on location in Noblesville, Carmel, and Indianapolis, Indiana

Business Supporters

Visit our supporters' websites. Buy their products/services. More info at
www.karmiccourage.com

bring Ingénue home

Ingénue on DVD at

www.karmiccourage.com

Twitter @ingenuemovie

Facebook www.facebook.com/ingenuemovie

Want Kate Chaplin to bring the film to your town for a special screening?

Email: kate@karmiccourage.com